THE DUCHESS HUNT

LOVE'S A GAME
BOOK ONE

VALERIE BOWMAN

JUNE THIRD ENTERPRISES, LLC

This is a work of fiction. Names, characters, places, and incidents are products of the author's imagination or are used fictitiously and are not to be construed as real. Any resemblance to actual events, locales, organizations or persons, living or dead, is entirely coincidental.

The Duchess Hunt, copyright © 2024 by June Third Enterprises, LLC.

All rights reserved. No part of this book may be reproduced in any form or by any electronic or mechanical means, including information storage and retrieval systems, without permission from the author, except for the use of brief quotations in a book review.

Print edition ISBN: 978-1-960015-26-6

Digital edition ISBN: 978-1-960015-25-9

Book Cover Design © Lyndsey Llewellen at Llewellen Designs.

school, and Meredith needed to grow up and make her debut. It was all a long way off. And if a "spare" son knew anything—spending his life waiting around to be noticed—it was patience. Griffin was exceedingly patient. He had no intention of declaring himself until the time was precisely right.

"I'm never going to marry," came Ash's voice from a little way down the bank. They'd been here all morning. Despite the fact that none of them had caught a thing, Ash was convinced that the fishing was better where he'd cast his line.

Meredith rolled her eyes at her brother's remark. "Of course you shall marry, Ash," she called back. "You'll be a marquess one day. You must produce an heir."

"You sound far too much like Father right now," Ash replied, scowling.

"But you *do* intend to marry one day, don't you, Griffin?" Meredith asked, blinking at him innocently.

"I do," Griffin replied, clearing his throat and steadfastly refusing to look at Meredith.

"Father says *I'm* to marry a *duke*," Meredith announced, squaring her shoulders and lifting her chin.

"A duke?" Griffin frowned. This was the first time he'd heard her say any such thing. Why was her father discussing such topics with her already? And why would he be so specific as to stipulate a duke? Surely, Lord Trentham didn't mean that literally. After all, Griffin was no duke.

"Father says a lot of things," Ash called with a frustrated sigh.

"He says I'm to marry a duke because that's what *Mama* would have wanted." Meredith's voice had taken on an edge of pride and wistfulness.

Griffin sat up straighter. He made a show of pulling his line from the water and adding fresh bait to his hook, but his mind raced. What the devil was Meredith talking about? Had her father really told her such a thing? Meredith revered the memory of her late mother. The Marchioness of Trentham had died in childbirth with Meredith, and the girl had spent her entire life trying to make her mother proud. Sadly, she tried to make her father proud too, while Ash had long ago stopped trying.

Lord Trentham was a complete horse's arse. Everyone knew that. Everyone except Meredith. After his wife's untimely death, Trentham had handed both children over to their nanny and left for London, where he spent all his time gambling and seeking his own pleasures. The nanny had later been replaced by a governess and a tutor, but Trentham had arranged it all from London. The man rarely came home. And when he did, it was heartbreaking to watch Meredith try so desperately to win the slightest hint of his approval and love.

Ash, for his part, mostly ignored his father. And now that the two boys were in school at Eton, Ash rarely had to deal with the man, which was precisely how Ash preferred it. The less contact, the better. Griffin and Ash were only here now on a break from school. An event Meredith always greatly looked forward to because, otherwise, she was here alone with only her governess and tutors as company.

"I don't think Mother said any such thing." Ash's voice sounded deep and angry. It always was when discussing anything related to his father.

"That's what Father said," Meredith shot back, lifting her chin again.

"Is your father home then?" Griffin asked, hoping to stave off an argument between the siblings while still trying to make sense of Meredith's surprising announcement.

"His lordship arrived last night," Ash drawled, looking none too pleased about his father's visit.

"That's why we're here," Meredith added. "We wanted to catch him some fish for supper."

"*You* want to catch him fish for supper. I simply enjoy fishing. Besides, it's not as if he'll notice where his supper came from." Disgust sounded in Ash's voice.

"I intend to tell him," Meredith said in a bright tone. "*If* we catch a fish, that is. Some dinner we'll have if we don't."

Griffin couldn't help himself. He didn't want to discuss fish at a time like this. He had to know more. "Which duke will you marry?" he asked Meredith, his brow still furrowed. "There aren't an infinite number of them, you know?"

Meredith shrugged. "I suppose I'll just have to see which dukes are eligible when I make my debut. I already know precisely how I want it to be." A happy smile popped to her lips. "I shall have a successful debut and be popular, but not too popular as I shouldn't want to be overwhelmed with offers."

Ash laughed and Meredith gave her brother a quelling look.

"I shall enjoy my Season immensely. And when I meet the man I'm going to marry, he will be tall and handsome. He'll come up to me at a ball and ask me to dance. He'll bow over my hand and call me 'My Lady.' He'll bring me flowers and take me for rides in the park."

Ash rolled his eyes, but Meredith was undeterred. "Then, just as I'm wondering whether he truly intends to offer, he shall invite me to the Cartwrights' Midsummer Night's ball, escort me out onto the balcony, fall to his knee, and tell me he loves me and ask me to marry him."

"That is *ridiculous* if you ask me," Ash grumbled, scratching his jaw and staring into the pond.

If Ash had been scoffing, Griffin had been listening with rapt attention. "But which duke would—?" Griffin began.

"I only know I shall *not* marry your brother," Meredith

said, wrinkling up her nose. "He's hideous." She shuddered slightly and frowned.

Griffin only nodded. Both Meredith and Ash knew Richard was hideous because Griffin had told them. Snobbish and full of himself, Richard had been taught by Griffin's father to act the part of a haughty duke from a young age. Griffin had often thought it sad that Richard was encouraged to be so lofty and condescending. He was never kind to Griffin. He called him "Spare" as a jest sometimes, but Richard mostly ignored Griffin the same way their father did. Griffin had long ago learned to pay no mind to his brother's jibes. Richard's teasing only grew worse if Griffin responded, and Richard never faced any consequences for his actions.

Griffin, however, was taken to task by his father for the slightest infraction. It was one of the many reasons he spent as little time as possible at home. He'd stopped longing for his brother's friendship and his father's attention.

Griffin had come to believe that being the spare was a relief, really. Anticipating a future as a duke came with a lot of nonsensical responsibility, if you asked him. Only now, with Meredith declaring that she would marry a duke one day, it was the first time in Griffin's life that he was even slightly envious of his older brother.

Griffin took a deep breath and flung his line back into the water. For the moment, there was no sense in worrying about Meredith's announcement. Like so many things, this situation also called for patience. There were many years before her debut. Plenty of time for things to change. Meredith just *couldn't* marry a duke. She had to marry *him*.

Because he loved her more than anything.

*For my niece, Clara Pikor.
Love, Aunt Vivi*

She wants to find his match…
Meredith Drake has sworn off marriage after her disastrous union with a much older man. But when her best friend returns from war, the young widow pledges to help him find his bride.

He wants to win her heart…
Griffin Brooks grew up as the 'spare' son, who no one noticed. He went to war to forget that Meredith was out of his reach. But now he's back, and no longer the 'spare.' With a dukedom at stake, he must take a bride. And for him, there is only one choice.

The hunt is on. Will true love be the prize?
When Meredith unexpectedly meets Griffin at a pleasure club and begins to see him in a whole new light, can he convince her to give passion…and love a chance?

PROLOGUE

Surrey, July 1803, The Marquess of Trentham's Estate

"Who do you think you shall marry, Griff?" asked Lady Meredith Drake as she tossed her fishing line back into the pond. The fourteen-year-old had just finished placing a fresh worm on her hook.

"Marry?" Griffin Brooks wrinkled his nose. "Why would I want to think about *that*? I'm only sixteen." Griffin shook his head, pulled his knees to his chest, and rested his arms atop them. He still clutched his fishing pole in his hand.

He adored his friend Meredith. She was one of the boys, as far as Griffin was concerned. But she'd begun asking him questions like this more often lately. Far too many probing questions about the future and things like marriage and Seasons and debut balls and the like. Subjects he had little interest in.

Griffin scrubbed a hand through his hair as he watched his line bob in the water. He and Mere were sitting on the grassy bank in front of the pond on Meredith's father's property. Meredith and her older brother, Ashford, were the only children of the Marquess of Trentham.

Griffin's own father, the Duke of Southbury, lived an hour's ride away. And while Griffin had an older brother who was eighteen and a younger sister who was only five, he rarely spent time at home. He much preferred to go riding by himself. One day, he'd made it all the way to the Drakes' estate, and when he returned home, no one had even noticed he'd been gone. After that he began making regular visits, and he was here so often these days he'd become part of the family.

At first, Griffin had befriended Ash, but it soon became obvious that precocious little Meredith refused to allow the boys to have all the fun. She accompanied them on all of their excursions and adventures. She was good at all the things they did, after all. It had seemed only natural. Now, Meredith could shoot as well as the two sixteen-year-old boys. She could fish. She could fence. And she could handle a horse better than most adult men. The three friends were inseparable and had been for as long as Griffin could remember. And all these years, Griffin thought of Meredith as nothing more than one of his two closest friends. What did it matter that she was a girl?

Only lately, he'd begun to notice that Meredith *was a girl*. In fact, she was quickly becoming a young woman. A *beautiful* young woman with her smokey-gray eyes and long dark-brown hair. And Griffin was increasingly uncomfortable with the thought that he'd begun to feel quite differently about Meredith. Quite differently indeed.

The truth was he hadn't answered her question because he already knew precisely who he would marry one day. It was simple. Like breathing. *Meredith*. He would marry Mere. It was the most effortless, obvious decision in the world.

But they were still quite young. He needed to finish

CHAPTER ONE

London, April 1816, The Duchess of Maxwell's Drawing Room

"It's time you take a wife, Griff," Meredith said as she poured herself a cup of tea.

Sitting across from her on the sofa, Griffin nearly spit the mouthful of tea he'd just ingested. "Pardon?" he managed to say as he coughed and spluttered. Thirteen years had passed. Were they *truly* still discussing his marriage prospects?

Meredith watched him from the corner of her eye. "I believe you heard me," she said with a sly smile as she dropped first one and then another lump of sugar in her cup.

Meredith had always adored sugar. After so many years in the army, Griffin had learned to live without it.

Griffin set down his cup and tugged at his neckcloth. The thing was choking him all of a sudden. He'd heard her all right. He merely couldn't believe what she'd said. "What's brought on this sudden desire to… to…?"

"See you married?" she supplied helpfully as she stirred her tea with a small silver spoon.

"Indeed."

"It's time, and you know it. Now that you're the duke, you have a responsibility to produce an heir. Not to mention that you promised your mother you'd take a wife the year you turn thirty." Meredith finished her explanation with a solid nod.

Griffin knew that nod. It was the nod that indicated she was right, and he could not argue with her. Well, he *could* argue with her, but he wouldn't win.

And she *was* right. Now that he was the blasted Duke of Southbury, he *did* need to produce an heir. Because Richard, his arse of an older brother—may he rest in peace—had failed to produce one before he'd gone and broken his idiotic neck during an inebriated horse race. Richard was inebriated. The horse was entirely clearheaded as far as Griffin knew.

"Am I thirty already?" he drawled, arching a brow at Meredith and allowing the hint of a smile to touch his lips. Anything to keep the subject off marriage. And hadn't he perfected making light of everything in front of Mere? Nothing was ever serious between them. Always light. Always a jest. Much easier that way.

He glanced over at Meredith. In the year since he'd been back from the war, Griffin, Meredith, and Ash had fallen easily back into their old friendship. It was almost as if Griffin *hadn't* been gone for over eight years. It was nearly as if Meredith *hadn't* married the old Duke of Maxwell at eighteen and become a widow last year at the age of six and twenty. It was practically as if Griffin *hadn't* completely ignored his brother's funeral and his father's demands that he return to London to stay safe since he'd become the heir to the dukedom. And it was not *quite* as if Griffin hadn't ignored his *father's* funeral two years ago and returned to London only after the war had ended and there was no one

THE DUCHESS HUNT

left to fight. In fact, despite his father's repeated insistence that Griffin return the moment he realized his "spare" was needed, Griffin had stayed through Waterloo. He earned the respect of the men who fought under him, his peers, his commanding officers, Parliament, and the King himself. But he *still* hadn't made Father proud. Of course not.

When Griffin came home, he'd half-hoped his feelings for Meredith would no longer be there. That the two of them could simply be friends, the way they had been when they'd first met. It would make everything much simpler.

Only he'd quickly realized that the years hadn't diminished his feelings for her at all. And even though they'd written to each other while he was gone, seeing her again had been like a punch to the gut, visceral and painful, nearly making him double over. Because while Meredith had been a lovely eighteen-year-old, the years had only enhanced her beauty. She'd grown into a more radiant woman than Griffin had ever imagined. And to this minute, his heart ached for her every time he saw her. Because if there was one thing Meredith had been clear on, not just in her letters but in everything she did and said since Griffin's return, it was her adamance that she would *never* marry again.

Meredith hadn't shared details of her marriage. Their letters had been filled with other things—gossip, frivolity, and commentary about Ash's latest foibles. But never anything too revealing. Never anything too unhappy. It was as if both Griffin and Meredith had an unspoken pact to only share the good parts of their lives, because the realities at the time had been too awful to impart.

And while Griffin knew very little about her marriage, he knew three things. Maxwell had spent most of his time in London, while Meredith remained in the country. They had never had a child. And as a result of whatever had happened between Meredith and her late husband, she abhorred the institution of marriage.

"You know you turn thirty this autumn," Meredith continued, pulling Griffin from his memories. "Your mother is at her wits' end. She's waited long enough, don't you think?"

Griffin expelled a long breath. Blast it. He *had* promised his mother he'd take a wife, but that promise had been made years ago, back when he'd been a soldier. Back when he'd assumed—no, hoped—he wouldn't even *live* through the war. He'd made the promise to his mother via letter. Of course, Mama, who adored Meredith, had immediately told her the news. And Meredith had the memory of an elephant. She forgot nothing. Neither did Mama. Which meant...he should have known this day was coming.

"Fine. What are you proposing?" Griffin said with another sigh, already aware he would regret asking.

"This is the year," Meredith announced after taking a sip of her tea. "With Gemma's debut this week, it's the perfect time. We're going out in Society. I've been out of mourning, and you've been back in London for nearly a year. In addition to helping Gemma make a match, it's time you find a wife. And I intend to help you *and* your sister. What's the point of being a duchess if you cannot help your friends?" There was that resolute nod again.

Ah, yes. *Friends*. They were *friends*. She reminded him of that often. He *wanted* to growl. Instead, he ensured that his voice sounded nothing but nonchalant. "Seems quite a lot to take on." He'd perfected it over the years, sounding completely indifferent about his emotions. An effect of being ignored as a child and madly in love with a woman who didn't love him back.

Meredith was right. This was the year. But not for her to help him find a wife. It was time for him to show Meredith they were perfect for each other. Endeavor to change her mind about marriage.

And he had a plan.

He'd never forgotten Meredith's dream to be courted, given flowers, and taken for rides in the park. Her dream had turned into a nightmare when her father had unceremoniously announced her betrothal to the old Duke of Maxwell at the start of her first Season. But Griffin intended to change all that. He intended to make her dream come true. He would ask her to marry him at the Cartwrights' annual Midsummer Night's Ball. Because if Griffin was going to marry, it *had* to be Meredith.

CHAPTER TWO

Five Nights Later, The Cranberrys' Ballroom

Meredith twirled in a circle as she took in the sights and sounds of the crowded space. She was wearing a new gown she'd commissioned specially for the occasion. Lavender silk with an empire waist and tiny circles embroidered along the hem and sleeves. Her hair was pinned atop her head in a chignon, and she wore white slippers and gloves, and a diamond necklace that had belonged to her mother.

Mama. The thought of her always made Meredith's throat tighten. What would Mama think of her now? Would she be proud that Meredith had become a duchess? Or would she be horrified that Meredith had failed as a wife by being unable to produce an heir to the Maxwell dukedom?

Meredith shook herself and forced a smile to her lips. This wasn't the time to be melancholy. Or to ruminate on the awful past. It was the first ball of the London Season. Exciting and full of promise, filled with debutantes and gentlemen in search of proper wives. And this year, darling

Gemma, Griffin's younger sister, was among them. Meredith adored Gemma, and she'd promised to help the girl navigate the Season. Meredith may not have had the courtship and marriage of *her* dreams, but she wished it for Gemma more than anything.

She knew exactly how Gemma felt, after all. The first ball of *Meredith's* first Season had been in this very place—the Cranberrys' ballroom. The family had hosted the first ball of the Season for as long as anyone could remember. Meredith glanced up at the chandelier filled with candles and, for a moment, it was as if she'd stepped back in time. Back to that night.

She'd been so full of hope. So convinced she would finally have a chance to prove herself to her father, to finally make him proud. She'd been planning to find the perfect suitor. A duke, just as Father had said. Just as Mama had wanted.

Meredith had set her sights on the Duke of Grovemont. He was handsome and young and from a good family with a large fortune. What's more, Ash and Griffin both liked him, and she trusted their judgement implicitly. She didn't know it that night, but she needn't have bothered trying to garner Grovemont's attention.

Not a sennight after her debut, Meredith was having supper with Father at his town house. Their dinners had become a regular occurrence since she'd come to London to prepare for the Season. In fact, Meredith had seen more of her father that month than she had the entirety of her childhood. She'd already decided that Society was ever so much more exciting than being stuck out in the countryside, alone. She was enjoying every moment of her first Season, just as she'd always known she would.

"Come to my study after dinner, Meredith," Father said as if it were an afterthought or something he'd just remembered. "There's something I need to speak to you about."

Meredith, of course, was certain he wanted to discuss her marriage prospects. She was dutifully prepared to tell him about her promising dance with the Duke of Grovemont at the Whitfields' ball the prior evening.

But when Meredith entered her father's study an hour later and took a seat in the large leather chair in front of his desk, he tossed a small stack of papers toward her and managed a tight, brief smile.

"There," he said, ever cryptic.

She pursed her lips and tipped her head to the side, not at all certain what he meant. "What is this?"

Father nodded at the papers. "It's all settled. You'll marry the Duke of Maxwell after the banns are read."

Meredith's heart plummeted to her stomach. "What?"

"The contract has been signed," Father reported.

Panic clawed at Meredith's insides. "But the Duke of Maxwell is...quite...old, is he not?" Her voice was high and thin, and she hated it.

"What does that have to do with it?" Father barked, narrowing his eyes on her, already disapproving.

"It's just that..." She searched her mind for the proper words. There had to be some way to make Father understand. "I barely know him. I don't—" She'd been about to say she didn't like what she did know about him. Not only was Maxwell old and unattractive, but there had also been rumors that he'd been cruel to his late wife. She'd died many years ago, but the rumors continued to swirl.

Her father impatiently slashed his hand through the air. "I thought you'd be pleased about this, Meredith. After all, you'll be a duchess. *It's what your mother wanted.*" He grabbed his lapels and stared at her, anger radiating from him in nearly palpable waves.

"Did Mama know the Duke of Maxwell?" Meredith ventured, still hating how timid her voice sounded.

THE DUCHESS HUNT

"What does that have to do with it? One duke is as good as the next. Maxwell's finances are in order. And he's willing to marry you. He doesn't seem to care that you do unladylike things like wear breeches and ride horses astride."

Meredith's cheeks burned. She'd spent her childhood knowing she wasn't exactly a proper young woman. But she'd had no one to show her. Other than her governess, who had been more interested in gossiping with the other servants than doing her job. As a result, Meredith had spent much of her youth gallivanting about the countryside with her brother and Griffin. She'd never considered how it might affect her marriage prospects. And if Father had been concerned about that, why hadn't he ever mentioned it?

She shook her head. There was no time to worry about that now. It took effort to breathe with the notion of marrying the elderly Duke of Maxwell encompassing her every thought. She had to think. Father had said one duke was as good as the next. Perhaps she should come at this a different way.

"I was hoping to catch the Duke of Grovemont's eye," she offered with a bright smile.

Her father scowled. "Grovemont's still a pup. And his family's holdings aren't as vast as Maxwell's."

Meredith swallowed hard. This couldn't be happening. Unwanted tears filled her eyes. "Yes, but—"

"But nothing. Maxwell it is." Father slammed his fist on the top of the desk, making the ominous stack of papers bounce.

Meredith folded her hands together in her lap and stared down at them. "But, Father, I don't want—"

Father leaned over the desk until his face was level with hers. Spittle flew from his lips. "What you want has nothing to do with this." His voice was hard and cold. His face had become a frightening mask. "You're my daughter and you'll do as you're told. The papers have already been signed."

Meredith swallowed hard and blinked back the tears that threatened to fall. She nodded slowly as the reality of the situation *filtered through her mind. Father was right. Her entire life, he'd only asked this one thing of her. And it was what Mama had wanted too. Hadn't Meredith always wanted to please Father? Hadn't she always wanted him to approve of her? To praise her for something? She would do as she was told.*

"Very well," *she said stoically. It wasn't as if she'd be the first or the last young woman to marry a man of her father's choosing. She had to be brave.* "I'll marry Maxwell."

Father's face transformed into a wide, satisfied smile, and relief spread through Meredith's veins. She'd finally done it. She'd finally made him happy. He'd never smiled at her before, she realized.

"Excellent," *Father said, straightening back to his full height.* "We'll have the banns read and put the announcement in the papers."

Father left the room whistling.
Meredith cried herself to sleep.

ASH HAD MADE a jest of it. Griffin had first tried to talk her out of it, then he'd *left*. But she'd gone through with the marriage, nonetheless. Of course, she'd gone on to be a colossal failure. She'd failed to do the one thing that was her sacred duty as a wife— produce an heir. Father had died a few years after her wedding. At least he hadn't lived to witness her shame.

Meredith shook her head to clear it of the unsettling thoughts of the past. Tonight wasn't about bad memories. Tonight was about Gemma's debut…and Griffin's impending betrothal. Her friends needed her help. Gemma was a dear, and she loved the girl as if she were her own sister. And Griffin, well, Griffin had been like a second brother to her for as long as she could remember.

Meredith was worried about Griff. She'd worried about

him for years, actually. Even though they'd had a row the night before he left—the night she'd told him about her betrothal to Maxwell—she'd spent endless nights praying for Griffin's safe return from the war.

He'd been different when he returned. There was no denying that. He'd had lines around the corners of his eyes, a permanent furrow to his brow, and he was far less quick to smile. But her dear friend was still there, and over the course of the past year, she'd been able to cajole him into laughing a bit more, enjoying himself a little...to remember the carefree, happy young man he'd once been.

Meredith had needed time too, of course. The years with Maxwell had taken their toll. To be sure, she hadn't been sad when her husband died, and she hadn't even felt guilty over her lack of grief. Awful of her, perhaps. But how could you mourn someone you barely knew? Someone who'd treated you like a stranger? Someone who harshly blamed you for failing to give him an heir?

No. She wouldn't think of it. Wouldn't think of *him*. That was all in the past, and it was high time both Meredith and Griffin stopped living in the past. They needed to enjoy themselves.

Griffin had an obligation to marry and produce an heir. He might not care about making his father proud, but his mother desperately wanted a grandchild. It was all she talked about. And Meredith and Griffin both loved the duchess very much.

As for Meredith enjoying herself...there was something else. Something she intended to do this Season. Something she hoped would clear away all the bad memories from her time with Maxwell. Something long overdue that she only planned to share with her *closest* friends. But first, she must see to Gemma and Griffin.

Meredith scanned the ballroom to find Gemma standing

in a large group of young ladies near the wall. The eighteen-year-old was wearing a white satin gown with pearls at her neck and matching pearl earbobs. Gemma was tall and willowy with short, curly dark hair and large, kind eyes. Gemma liked to say that she was awkward. That she was too tall, her neck far too long, her eyes far too large for her face, and that her hair was an unruly mess. But she'd been assured repeatedly by her mother that the women in their family took a bit longer than others to come into their beauty. They all expected that once she blossomed, Gemma would be more beautiful than they could imagine. In the meantime, her lack of classical beauty didn't bother Gemma in the least. Perpetually happy, the girl had decided to devote herself this Season to enjoying herself and helping her many friends find agreeable matches. It was so like Gemma to think of others before herself. She had the most fiercely loyal, kind heart of anyone Meredith had ever known, and that, of course, was far more important than physical beauty.

Gemma came galloping over and stopped in front of Meredith, tapping her foot on the parquet floor.

"You won't believe what's happened," Gemma announced, crossing her arms over her chest. The girl had a fierce look in her eye that Meredith recognized immediately. The Southbury Stubborn Streak.

"What's wrong, darling?" Meredith reached out to touch Gemma's gloved elbow.

"Lady Mary Costner, that's what's wrong," Gemma nearly growled.

Meredith narrowed her eyes. She'd heard that name before and it was never associated with anything good. "What did Lady Mary do?"

"She's threatened all the other debutantes. She told all the girls that if she sees them dancing with any of the most eligible bachelors, she will spread rumors about them and ruin their reputations."

Meredith frowned, letting her hand fall back to her side. "You can't be serious."

"I wish I wasn't. Hideous girl. Who does she think she is?" Gemma plunked her gloved fists on her narrow hips.

Meredith glanced over to the large group of debutantes huddled against the wall. "Is that why all the young ladies are flocked together this evening?"

"Yes." Gemma nodded. "I intend to do something about it."

Warning bells sounded in Meredith's head. "Gemma, be careful," she advised. "These sorts of things can become messy. Scandal has a way of finding even the most unlikely victim." Meredith was thinking of her own dear friend, Clare Handleton. Clare knew all too well how quickly a scandal could ruin a debutante.

"I'll be careful," Gemma agreed, "but I refuse to let Lady Mary intimidate me. I intend to rally the troops to dance with *all* the eligible gentlemen!" Gemma declared before lifting her skirts and hurrying off in the direction of the wallflowers.

Meredith watched her go, biting her lip. Gemma always meant well, but she had the same stubbornness Griffin did when she made up her mind about something. And unlike Griffin, Gemma was exceedingly impatient.

Meredith should discuss the situation with Gemma's mother. She turned to search the ballroom for the older woman, but she found Griffin standing in front of her. A smile popped to her lips. "There you are, Griff."

Griffin was dressed in his best. All black evening attire with a white shirtfront and waistcoat and a perfectly starched snowy cravat. His dark eyes were shining with mischief, and it looked as if he'd just recently scrubbed a hand through his thick, dark hair. He was so tall and fit and handsome. It was entirely unfair of him to be so good-looking *and* an eligible duke. He would make some fortunate lady an excellent husband.

"I'm sorry I'm late," Griffin said. "I was speaking to some friends across the room. I just saw Gemma leave. Is she enjoying herself?"

Meredith sighed. "I'm afraid she's taking it upon herself to champion the wallflowers."

Griffin shook his head. "That sounds like Gemma."

"Yes, well, I intend to speak with your mother about it later, but since you're here…" She gave Griffin a sly smile.

"Why are you looking at me like that?" His deep voice was filled with suspicion.

"Like what?" She shrugged innocently.

Griffin narrowed his eyes on her. "Like I'm the first prize at the county fair."

Meredith threw back her head and laughed. "You just might be. You are, after all, an eligible duke, one who is looking for a wife this Season. And you are in the middle of a *ton* ball."

He winced. "Which means?"

"Which means…" Meredith clapped her hands together. "Let the duchess hunt begin."

CHAPTER THREE

"The duchess hunt, eh? Is *that* what we're calling it?" Griffin scratched the back of his neck as he eyed Meredith up and down.

Meredith looked gorgeous tonight, as usual. He'd barely been able to take his eyes off of her since he'd spotted her across the ballroom earlier. If he hadn't been waylaid by friends, he would have made his way to her side before now.

"Why not?" Meredith replied, a sparkle in her eye. One he remembered well from their childhood. "Don't we love to make everything into a competition?"

Griffin tugged at his cuff and allowed a half-smile to curl his lips. "It's a competition now, is it?"

Meredith shrugged one shoulder in that adorable way of hers. "I don't see why it shouldn't be. I'll choose some ladies for you, and you choose some for yourself, and we'll see who does the better job of it."

Griffin's smile widened. He couldn't help it. It was just like Meredith to assume she could find a better wife for him than he could. Of course, why she'd never thought of herself was cause for concern. He intended to change that, however.

To get her to notice him...as a man. A man who wanted her. A man who would do anything for her. *Patience*.

"What about Gemma?" he asked in a blatant attempt to change the subject. "I thought you were intent on helping *her* find a husband?"

Meredith knocked her shoulder against his and gave him a sardonic smile. "One of the amazing things about me is that I can do more than one thing at a time."

Griffin tried not to react as he breathed in her bergamot-scented perfume. It did something to him...every time. Made the muscles in his abdomen tighten. He'd missed it all those years on the Continent. Missed it but *never* forgot it.

"And don't think I don't know you're simply trying to change the subject," Meredith continued, still smiling at him.

"Me?" He pointed at his chest. "Never." She knew him too well.

Meredith laughed, and the sound rolled over him like sunlight glancing off the top of a pond on a bright morning. Meredith's laugh was the best sound in the world. The memory of it had kept him sane during some dark, dark days.

"Yes, well, the fact is that your incorrigible little sister has apparently decided to become the de facto leader of the wallflowers against a particularly nasty chit named Lady Mary Costner. Seems she's more interested in that at the moment than husband-hunting."

While Griffin frowned, Meredith briefly recapped what Gemma had told her.

"Let me see if I have the right of it. Lady Mary threatened them with...spreading rumors?" Griffin asked after Meredith finished.

"Apparently." Meredith sighed.

"And Gemma has vowed not to stand for it?" Griffin

continued as he grabbed two champagne flutes off the tray of a passing footman. He handed one to Meredith.

"Yes."

"Well done, Gemma." Griffin proudly lifted his champagne glass in the semblance of a toast to his sister. "Of course, Gemma's not intimidated by that girl. She's a Southbury."

Meredith took a sip from her flute. "I'm worried she'll do something impetuous."

"Like we did when we were her age?" Griffin drawled, catching Meredith's eyes and holding her gaze.

"Precisely like we did when we were her age," Meredith replied, lifting her brows and returning Griffin's gaze with a sly smile.

Griffin shook his head. "I'm not worried. Gemma is clever. She won't do anything to ruin her reputation. Though I must say, it all sounds like a lot of dramatic nonsense to me, but what do I know about the marriage mart?" He sighed.

"Precisely," Meredith replied with that firm nod. "Which is why I intend to help you find a suitable bride."

"Must you?" Griffin asked smoothly as he brought his champagne glass to his lips again. He knew Meredith well enough to know that she would not take no for an answer. Not easily at least. Which is why he had a plan.

Meredith took charge of things like a general on a battlefield. There was only one way to handle her. By catching her off guard. The element of surprise was required. Fortunately, Griffin had had several days to contemplate his strategy. He was fully prepared.

"Of course I must." Meredith was already surveying the large group of supposed wallflowers, obviously in an attempt to find the best of the Season's young ladies.

"Lady Hannah Hartley is lovely," Meredith began, lifting

her chin toward a petite blonde young woman wrapped in a mess of pink chiffon.

"Mmm," was Griffin's only reply as he took another sip from his glass.

"Miss Eagerton is quite accomplished. But I fear her name is too accurate, as she seems to be staring at you already."

"Hmm," Griffin replied with long-practiced nonchalance. He didn't return Miss Eagerton's stare.

"Miss Barton is very pretty, and I've heard she's a quick wit. A good choice for you."

"I do like a woman with a quick wit," Griffin replied, the edge of his mouth quirking up.

"And I should like it too. We don't want anyone who isn't witty."

"We?" He drew out the word, arching a brow.

"Yes. You don't expect me to stop being your friend just because you marry. I must ensure your bride is someone I will enjoy spending time with as well."

Griffin nearly laughed aloud at that, while Meredith continued her narrow-eyed assessment of the ballroom's female occupants.

"You're wasting your time, Mere," he finally said, scrubbing his hand through the back of his hair.

"I am not. This is the perfect place to find your duchess and you know it." Meredith lifted on her tiptoes as if to get a better look at the debutantes. "Lady Mary Costner is obviously not to be considered."

"Obviously," Griffin agreed. "But there's no need to continue naming young ladies. I have every intention of settling down. But not until the correct woman says yes."

"I know," Meredith said impatiently, continuing her search. "That's *why* I'm helping you to find the perfect match."

Griffin took another sip of champagne. "But as I said, you're wasting your time."

Meredith lowered herself to the balls of her feet, turned to him, and frowned. "That's the second time you've said that. Why, precisely, do you believe I'm wasting my time?"

"Because I already know who I shall ask to marry me. I simply haven't asked her yet."

CHAPTER FOUR

Meredith sucked in her breath so sharply she nearly choked. She must not have heard him correctly. Because it certainly sounded as if Griffin Brooks, her best friend since childhood, her closest companion, had just said that he *already knew* who he would marry.

But that wasn't possible. Meredith knew everything about him. She knew he liked to wake up early and go riding in the park. She knew he liked his coffee and tea without milk or sugar. She knew he was terribly kind to his servants, and they all adored him.

There were no surprises between them. Why, Griffin even knew she hadn't shed a single tear when her late husband died. There was only one thing she'd never told him. A thing she had no intention of telling him. But it simply wasn't possible that Griffin had a lady in mind to marry and *Meredith* was not aware.

"For Christ's sake, *who?*" came flying out of her mouth before she had a chance to craft her question in a more eloquent fashion.

THE DUCHESS HUNT

Griffin smiled and shook his head, while Meredith cleared her throat and sheepishly glanced around to ensure no one had overheard her indelicate speech.

Griffin's grin was positively smug. "I have no intention of telling *you*."

Her brows snapped together, and her mouth popped open. "What? Why not? Whatever can you mean? Why *wouldn't* you tell me?" What was he about teasing her this way? Couldn't he surmise that she was about to have an apoplectic fit in the middle of the Cranberrys' ballroom?

"Because you are the sort who would march directly up to the lady and announce it, and I plan to be much more subtle than that."

Meredith's shoulders were so tight she thought they might squeeze her ears. She plunked both hands on her hips. "Are you seriously telling me that finally, after all these years, you fancy a lady and you refuse to tell me who she is?"

He bit his lip in that boyish way of his and glanced at her from beneath his long, thick lashes. "That's precisely what I'm telling you."

Her nostrils flared, and she lifted her chin. "You know I cannot bear that answer."

"Of course I know." He brought his champagne glass to his lips again.

The furrow between her brows deepened. "You know I shall not be able to *live* with that answer."

His shrug was positively infuriating. "Be that as it may."

"How cruel can you be?" she asked, fully prepared to resort to dramatics if she must.

He arched a brow at her. "You know as well as I do that you cannot keep a secret to save your own life. If I'm to have any finesse whatsoever in executing a proper courtship, I cannot tell you, Mere. It's that simple."

Meredith *wanted* to stamp her foot. She *wanted* to beg him to tell her. She briefly considered socking him in the gut for torturing her. But her years of ladylike behavior—the behavior she'd had to painstakingly teach herself by watching other ladies go about in Society — were drilled into her now and could not be denied. Instead, she closed her eyes briefly, pressed her lips together firmly, and opened her eyes once more. "Very well. I shall allow that I cannot keep a secret." Most secrets, that is. Of course, Griffin had no way of knowing there was *one* secret she'd kept for years. She'd never told him she was barren. It was too humiliating.

"Good. Then I can expect you to stop asking me who she is?"

"You must be jest—" Wait. No. That was not the way to handle Griffin. When he made up his mind about something, there was no reasoning with him. The Southbury Stubborn Streak was nothing to discount. She blew out a deep breath, straightened her shoulders, and lowered her voice. "Very well. What if I *guess*?"

His dark brows shot up. "Guess?"

She smoothed her hand down her lavender gown with practiced nonchalance. She mustn't seem too excited or he would certainly say no. They had always been competitive. This would be nothing more than another one of their many competitions. A game. "Yes. What if I guess who she is? Will you tell me then?"

Griffin rubbed his chin with his forefinger. His eyes narrowed, and he appeared to contemplate the matter for a moment. "Hmm."

"Oh, you must tell me, Griff. If I guess, that is. Otherwise, I shall just die. I will simply perish." Nonchalance had never been her strong suit.

He side-eyed her. "You're that confident you can guess the lady's identity, are you?"

Was that a real question? "Of course I am."

She was not. But she also wasn't about to tell him that. And regardless, she would just keep guessing until she worked it out.

He poked out his cheek with his tongue. "Very well. I shall allow you to guess…with one caveat."

She scowled at him. She didn't like caveats.

He chuckled. "Don't look so disgruntled. I'm giving you a chance, aren't I?"

She folded her arms across her chest. "Fine. What is your caveat?"

"You may only have seven guesses."

This time, she did stamp her foot. "But that's not—"

"Ah, ah, ah." He waggled a finger in front of her face. "That's my condition. Accept it or don't. Seven guesses. No more. No less. Otherwise, you'll guess every woman in England."

Thwarted. Her eyes narrowed to slits. Of course Griffin was too clever to allow her an infinite number of guesses. "Fine. I accept." She turned toward the ballroom and surveyed its occupants with a shrewd eye. "Now. Who shall be my first guess?"

CHAPTER FIVE

The Next Morning, Gentleman Jack's Boxing Saloon

"Will you *please* just tell my sister you're madly in love with her and have been for years?" Ashford Drake said as he swung a fist directly at Griffin's head.

Griffin ducked, narrowly missing the hit. Damn Ash. Not only did the man have a mean left hook, he was also far too astute. He'd guessed Griffin's feelings for Meredith long ago and while he had sworn to keep the secret, it didn't stop him from bringing it up to Griffin when they were alone. *Nearly every time they were alone.*

Ash was a tall, strapping man who shared his sister's dark-brown hair, light-gray eyes, and penchant for being forthright. Ash would do anything for a friend in need, and Griffin trusted him with his life. Which is how he knew the marquess would never share his secret. He would take it to the grave if need be.

The two men had been boxing for the better part of an hour, and Griffin had just finished telling Meredith's older brother about how set she was on helping him find a bride. Hence Ash's question.

"You know perfectly well why I haven't told her yet," Griffin returned, landing a solid blow to his friend's right side. He enjoyed that particular hit a bit more than usual.

Ash grunted and repositioned his bare fists. "I know why you *say* you don't tell her, but I still contend it's ludicrous." He swung at Griffin and missed.

"You mean it's romantic."

Another swing. Another miss. "For God's sake, man, why wait? Just tell her the next time you see her."

Another undercut to Ash's right side that landed with a solid *thwunk*. "Patience is a virtue."

"Patience is boring," Ash shot back with a groan.

"Spoken like a man without a drop of patience in his veins. Look. The situation must be handled delicately. You know as well as I do that Meredith has sworn off marriage. She says she *detested* it."

Breathing heavily, Ash bobbed on his feet, no doubt looking to attempt one of his vicious left hooks again. "She detested *Maxwell*."

Griffin bobbed too, just barely dodging the punch when it came. Ash was correct, but Griffin knew Meredith's aversion to marriage involved more than simply a bad match with Maxwell. Something had happened in her marriage. Something she refused to talk about. He could only hope that once she realized they were the perfect couple, once she realized how much he loved her, Meredith would open up to him about it. *Patience. Patience.* "It's complicated," he said.

Ash rolled his eyes. Patience was anathema to him. The marquess had never encountered anything so complicated he couldn't just barrel in and accomplish it. He made decisions quickly and worried about the consequences later. So, of course, Ash made it sound simple. Just tell the woman you love her, and everything will fall perfectly into place.

Ash was a good man and a great friend, but he would never understand. He might be a marquess in need of an heir, but like his sister, he was completely uninterested in marriage. Griffin suspected he was set against marriage to spite his dead father. Which was really something when you thought about it. The man was *no longer alive*.

The truth was that, sadly, Ash didn't understand the meaning of the word "love." Not when it came to marriage. Ash saw marriage as little more than a business arrangement. It wasn't his fault, of course. He'd grown up in a house devoid of that emotion. Griffin knew firsthand how cold Ash's steely-eyed father had been. At least Griffin had been loved by his mother. He knew love. And he had no intention of marrying if Meredith refused to be his wife. He didn't want to live a life without her, *and* it would be unfair to marry any other woman. But Griffin wouldn't bother trying to explain his feelings to Ash. Such things just didn't make sense to the marquess.

"Tell me again *why* it's so complicated," Ash said with another eyeroll.

"It just is," Griffin replied, missing Ash this time with another right undercut.

Ash expelled his breath as he circled Griffin. "Of course it is. You and Meredith both always seem to complicate *everything*."

"Easy for you to say. You've never been in love," Griffin replied with his practiced nonchalance.

"And thank God for that," Ash said with a grin as he continued to circle him. "Tell me. How much longer do you intend to live in agony?"

Griffin wiped his forearm across his sweaty brow. "I have a plan."

Still sweating and bobbing, Ash smiled and shook his head. "Of course you do."

"What's wrong with having a plan?"

Sweat beaded down Ash's bare chest as he bobbed and weaved around the space. "Sounds complicated again." He let out a long, loud groan. "I swear you're both wasting valuable time. And what do you intend to tell her now that she's so hell-bent on your marriage this Season? I had dinner with her the other night and it's nearly all she talked about."

A bell sounded from the corner, indicating their bout was through. Griffin expelled his breath. He dropped his fists and jogged over to the wall to get water and a towel from the bottle man. Ash followed him.

"All part of my plan," Griffin said, taking a large swallow of water. "I already told her that I know precisely who I intend to marry."

Ash's brows shot up. "Really?" Ash took a swig from his own bottle.

"I just didn't tell her who."

"Really?" Ash repeated before a sly smile spread across his face. "That must have gone over like a ship's anchor."

Griffin scrubbed the towel across his sweaty face. "She has seven guesses."

Ash rolled his eyes and rubbed his forehead with one knuckle. "See? Complicated. What if she guesses herself?"

Griffin shrugged. He'd thought of that. Of course he'd thought of it. "I hope she does. If she guesses herself, it will mean she's open to the idea," he finished with a grin. "Otherwise, I intend to court her properly and ask her to marry me at the Cartwright's Midsummer Night's Ball."

Ash shook his head again, blowing out his breath in a rush. "You are *mad*, you know that?"

"Perhaps, but I intend to handle this my way. Besides, I doubt she'll guess herself."

"This is all *far* too complicated, if you ask me. What if I make it easier for you? If you tell Meredith you love her before the Cartwrights' ball, I'll agree to find a bride before my thirty-*first* birthday."

Griffin grinned at his friend and shook his head. "You? The forever-sworn bachelor? Marry?"

Ash's sly smile returned. "Ah, but that's how certain I am that you *won't* tell her."

Griffin shook his head. That was Ash. Never a care in the world. Never a problem he couldn't solve. The quintessential devil-may-care rake about town. It was impossible not to like him.

"I hope to see you fall in love one day," Griffin said as he and Ash headed for the back of the saloon, where a makeshift showering system had been set up behind curtains with buckets, water, and barrel tubs. "Then perhaps you'll know how difficult it is."

Ash's crack of laughter bounced off the high, plastered ceiling. "I'll tell you one thing. If I *am* unfortunate enough to fall in love someday, you can rest assured that I will come out and tell the lady my feelings. I'd much rather be rejected than subject myself to years of torment the way you have."

Griffin gently elbowed his friend in the ribs. "Care to place a wager on that?"

CHAPTER SIX

The Next Morning, The Duchess of Maxwell's Breakfast Room

"And not only did she dance with Lord Pembroke, one of the *most* eligible bachelors of the Season, but she told Lady Mary if she dared to utter a word against her, she'd start an equally damaging rumor about *her*," Meredith said, finishing the story she was telling Clare Handleton over scones. "Oh, how I wished you'd been there. Not only would you have loved to see Gemma in action, but I daresay you would have helped to thwart that awful Lady Mary," Meredith finished with a nod.

A catlike smile popped to Clare's bow-shaped lips. "Yes, one cannot underestimate the value of a well-timed slide of the foot to trip a particularly unpleasant chit," she finished with a saucy wink.

Meredith laughed. "Indeed."

"Quite brave of Gemma, but I do hope you shared my story with her. A reputation is nothing to take for granted," Clare continued as she picked through some grapes on her plate. "Take it from *Scandalton*. *Not* that I give a toss about any of it these days."

Meredith reached over and squeezed her friend's hand. It was one of the many things she loved about Clare. She was fabulous and fearless, the bravest woman Meredith knew. Clare *should* have been at the Cranberrys' ball. She *should* be married and the mother of several adorable children by now. But Clare had been involved in a huge scandal the year she and Meredith had debuted. It was the reason she'd been given that awful nickname by the more horrid members of the *ton*. The scandal—and the nickname—had even made it to the papers.

And now Clare was a twenty-seven-year-old self-proclaimed spinster, who no longer attended any Society events. Instead, Clare was stuck with her elderly mother, who, even after all these years, sniped at her only child constantly for ruining her chances. Meredith could barely stand to think of it. Her friend's fate had been so utterly unfair. The man who'd ruined her had not faced any consequences whatsoever.

Clare and her mother were in town for a short visit. They never stayed for the entire Season. They simply did some shopping, endured gossip from those who saw them on the streets, and returned to their little enclave in the country. But Meredith looked forward to Clare's visits. Meredith used them as an opportunity to try to persuade Clare to make an appearance in Society, which her friend always graciously declined. Of course, Meredith understood Clare's reticence. Society was a cruel, cold place for a woman who had dared break its rules.

At least Meredith was able to see her good friend upon occasion. Meredith loved her and the two had remained steadfast friends all these years. Meredith had been Clare's only remaining friend after her name had been tarnished.

Clare was blond, with intelligent dark-brown eyes and a mischievous smile. Despite what she'd been through, Clare was still quick to laugh, and her positive demeanor was one of the many things Meredith loved about her. That and her quick wit.

Clare had left her mother at home this morning, thank heavens, and had only brought her maid along as a chaperone. The maid was down in the kitchens visiting with the other servants while the ladies talked. Which suited Meredith's purposes just fine. There was something she wanted to tell her closest friend. The something she'd been thinking about for several weeks now. The something she dared not write in a letter.

Clare's hearty laugh filled the room. "I'm so pleased to hear that Gemma didn't let that awful girl ruin her evening. What else did I miss at this Season's opening ball?" Clare asked as she took a sip from the teacup Meredith had just handed her.

Meredith waggled her eyebrows at her friend. She'd been waiting for this particular question all morning. "You'll never believe it, but *Griffin* has agreed to finally choose a bride this Season. Or I suppose I should say he's already chosen her."

"Pardon?" Clare's brows shot up. "Griffin? Chose a bride? You *must* be jesting."

Meredith took a sip from her teacup. "I reminded him that he promised his mother that he would marry the year he turns thirty."

"And here I was assuming that was merely something one tells one's mother when one is not yet thirty," Clare replied, grinning.

"Yes, well, it seems he was quite serious. And you could have knocked me over with a feather, but he told me he's already decided who he intends to ask to marry him."

"*Who?*" Clare nearly shouted as she leaned forward, obviously on tenterhooks to hear more. She popped a grape into her mouth.

"That's just it. He refuses to tell me who she is. He is, however, allowing me to guess. Though I've already used my first guess and I was wrong."

Clare's brows drew together. "Guess? Whatever do you mean?"

Another sip of tea. "He's given me seven chances to guess the identity of the lady of his choosing."

Clare laughed. "Only seven? That doesn't seem terribly wise of him. He has to know that if you fail to guess correctly, you'll never stop nagging him about it."

Meredith laughed. "That is true, but I should hope by the time I use up all my guesses, he'll be properly courting this woman, and her identity shall become obvious."

"That is curious." Clare pursed her lips and tapped them with her fingertip. "Who do you think she is?"

"I've no idea, but I know she's *not* Amelia Barnstaple because I guessed her name at the Cranberrys' ball. Which means I have six guesses left."

Clare scowled and shook her head. "I cannot picture Griffin with Amelia Barnstaple. Far too simple for him."

"Perhaps," Meredith allowed.

"How long has this been going on? Why hasn't Griffin already told you about her?" Clare wanted to know.

Meredith began nodding. "Precisely what I thought when he first mentioned it. Honestly. How could he keep such news from me?"

Clare continued to tap her fingertip against her bottom lip. "Who *is* she?"

Meredith cocked her head to the side and considered the mystery lady's identity for the thousandth time. "I honestly don't know. In fact, I had no idea he fancied anyone. Who do *you* see him with?"

A sly smile curved Clare's lips as she picked up her teacup. "Honestly?"

Meredith blinked at her friend, studying her face. "Of course."

Clare lifted one shoulder in the semblance of a shrug. "I've always pictured him with *you*, Mere."

Meredith nearly dropped her teacup into her lap. She fumbled with placing it on the tabletop in front of her. "Me?"

Clare sipped her tea. "You two are together all the time. Thick as thieves."

"We're *friends*. Close *friends*," Meredith said hastily, blurting out the words as if attempting to convince herself as much as Clare. The memory of Griffin standing so tall and handsome beside her last night floated through her mind. There couldn't be a woman alive who didn't find Griffin handsome, and he smelled divine too, but that was beside the point. He was Griffin. Her best friend.

"You must admit you make a good-looking pair." Clare twirled a hand in the air. "You laugh at the same jests. You enjoy the same pastimes. What else would make a happy marriage?"

Compatibility...in bed.

The thought made Meredith's mouth go dry. The image of Griffin in bed was... Wait. She shook her head. What was Clare saying? She? And Griffin? A ludicrous notion.

"I never intend to marry again. You know that," Meredith hurried to add. How many times had she repeated that same sentence to anyone who brought up the subject of her ever pairing off again?

Clare continued, fluttering her hand in the air. "I know. I know. But you asked who I pictured Griffin with, and I answered." Another shrug.

"And even if I wanted to..." Meredith let her voice drift off.

"I know, Mere." Clare's voice was filled with sympathy as she reached over and patted her hand. Clare knew her secret, that Meredith was unable to bear children. And she knew that was one of the reasons she would never marry again. She would not saddle a man with a wife who couldn't bear children. But it was also the reason for her *other* secret. The one she was dying to tell Clare. The one she'd been planning to reveal for weeks now. The one she intended to tell Clare just as soon as the conversation allowed.

Quickly changing the subject like the dear that she was, Clare went on to recite several amusing stories about her time in the country with her mother, but Meredith barely heard them. Something else had filled her mind. She? And Griffin? No. Definitely ludicrous. For heaven's sake, just the very thought was…well, it was…disconcerting at best.

"I cannot believe he fancies a lady and hasn't told me who," Meredith finally blurted.

"Are we talking about Griffin again?" Clare asked, blinking.

"Yes, sorry." Meredith bit her lip. "It's just distracting me to no end."

"I can see that," Clare replied, slowly lifting a brow. "Tell me. Does he love her?"

Meredith blinked again and frowned. "Love who?"

"This woman Southbury intends to ask to marry him. Does he love her?"

"I… why… I didn't ask him that." Meredith clapped her mouth shut. Oh, dear. *That* was a new thought. Why hadn't she asked him? He'd said he knew who he would propose to. Love had never been mentioned. But now that she thought on it, *did* Griffin love this woman? Her eyes narrowed. Who was she? And why did it suddenly matter so much that Meredith find out *immediately*?

Clare sighed and stretched her arms above her head. "Oh, it's so nice to be out of mother's sight even for an hour or two."

"How is your mother?" Meredith asked, only to be polite. And Clare knew it.

Another sigh. "Oh, Mother is Mother." She rolled her eyes. "How is your brother?"

Meredith smiled. "Oh, you know Ash. Always fine. Never any problems. Always having fun."

Clare took another sip of tea. "At least *someone's* having fun. What about Ash? Is *he* planning to take a wife this year? He turns thirty as well, doesn't he?"

Meredith rolled her eyes. "I think it shall take more than a birthday to convince Ashford Drake to take a wife. You know he's publicly declared he has no intention of marrying. Ever."

"In front of the King, no less," Clare said, shaking her head and laughing. "Not exactly the proper way to remain in the good graces of the monarch."

Meredith shrugged. "Ash doesn't give a toss. He never has."

Clare's smile was bright. "We have that in common. I suppose that's why I've always liked him." Clare sighed and stood. "I must be going. Mama will have a conniption if I'm gone too long. You must write me as soon as you discover the identity of Southbury's mysterious lady. It's far too interesting of a tale, and it's far too boring in the country."

"Rest assured, you'll be the second to know after *I* find out. But you cannot go yet," Meredith declared. "There's something else I need to tell you. Something important. Something…private."

"Ooh, well then. Let Mama have a conniption. It'll be good for her," Clare said as she immediately fell back into her seat and leaned forward. "What is it?"

Meredith bit her lip. "I have plans this Season too."

"What sort of plans?" Clare asked, waggling her eyebrows.

Meredith cleared her throat. She had not come to this decision lightly, but it would be real if she said it aloud. And Clare was the perfect person to tell first. Meredith closed her eyes briefly and blurted, "I intend to take a lover."

Clare's brows shot straight up, but then a sly smile covered her face. "Really?"

"Yes. And you're the one who gave me the idea. Last time we spoke."

"Really?" Clare's brows remained raised. "Remind me. What exactly did I say?"

"You said, 'Marriage and sex are two different things. No one knows that better than I do. One is certainly not dependent on the other.'"

"Well, *that's* true," Clare replied with a snort-laugh.

"And I...I never felt as if Maxwell and I...well, it was *not* fulfilling."

"I don't doubt it," Clare continued, shaking her head.

Meredith winced. The truth was that Maxwell's lovemaking had consisted of slobber-filled kisses and unceremonious breast-grabbing. Then he'd rolled atop her and, well, she hadn't felt much. Just some ineffective thrusting before he rolled off of her and cursed her for some failing on her part that she didn't exactly understand. All she really did know was that none of it had been pleasant.

But she'd heard ladies talk about passion. She'd read books that acclaimed it. For more than one reason, she would never marry again, but she was *eager* to take a lover. What would it feel like to have a young, handsome virile man atop her? What would it feel like to actually *want* to go to bed with a man, be touched by him, touch him back? The thought sent a delicious shiver through her.

"It's high time you did this," Clare was saying as she picked up her teacup and held it out in front of her. "No doubt I shall hear no end of it from Mother when I return, but pour me another cup of tea, Your Grace, and *do tell me more*. I'm quite happy to help you plan everything."

CHAPTER SEVEN

The Next Evening, The Rothschilds' Ballroom

"You cannot expect to court a lady if you're spending all your time at *my* side," Meredith explained to Griffin as they strolled through the crowded ballroom arm in arm.

Tonight, she was wearing one of her favorite gowns, a lovely pink concoction with tiny roses embroidered along both the hem and empire waist. Her hair was swept up in a dark chignon, and she'd finished the ensemble with Mama's diamond necklace and earbobs.

One of the things Meredith loved best about being a widow was the ability to go nearly anywhere, wear whatever she liked, and do mostly what she liked. There was such freedom in widowhood it had nearly been worth the awful years of her marriage. Nearly. At any rate, it felt good to be back in Society, to no longer have to worry about her failure to give the Duke of Maxwell an heir. She was done worrying about Maxwell's condemnation. It was time to live for herself. And she was ready. Which was precisely why she'd decided to take a lover. A small grin popped to her lips the way it always did when she thought of it.

Just as she'd suspected, Clare hadn't judged her at all. To the contrary, she'd been a fountain of knowledge. Who knew her scandal-ridden friend would have such information to impart? Clare had been the first and only person who Meredith had told of her wicked plans. But tonight, she intended to inform Griffin as well. But for some reason, her stomach was in knots over it. Why did she have the feeling Griffin wouldn't be quite as approving?

"Who says I'm beginning my courtship tonight?" Griffin replied from her side, jarring her from her scandalous reverie.

As usual, Griffin looked handsome as sin. Tall and dark, he wore all black evening attire that was perfectly fitted and a snowy white shirt front and matching cravat that was expertly and effortlessly tied. Griffin always wore the finest clothing, and he did it while simultaneously giving the impression that he had barely tried.

"*I've always pictured him with* you, *Mere.*" Clare's words niggled at Meredith's mind. Truthfully, she'd been unable to sleep last night for thinking about them. She and Griffin? No. The notion was ludicrous. *Ludicrous.*

Of course Griffin was handsome, and tall, and fit, and muscled, and clever, and funny, and wise and…well, everything a woman would want in a man…a partner. But that was just it. Meredith wasn't looking for a partner. She wasn't looking for a husband. She was in the market for a lover, and she would never jeopardize her friendship with Griffin for a few (or even many) sinful nights of pleasure. Not to mention, that wouldn't be fair to Griffin's future wife. And Griffin needed a wife. He needed an heir. And Meredith could not give him either.

Besides, he'd already indicated that he had a lady in mind.

Griffin was about to make some fortunate young woman's dreams come true. And that was what they should concentrate on tonight.

Meredith surveyed the crowd filled with beautiful, well-dressed ladies. Who? Who did Griffin fancy? Not knowing had been slowly driving her mad all week. But the even greater mystery was did he *love* this woman? That question had haunted Meredith ever since Clare had asked it. But for some reason, the thought of hearing his answer made her uneasy.

"*Aren't* you beginning your courtship?" Meredith replied, intent on keeping her thoughts firmly where they belonged —on the hunt for Griffin's duchess. Meredith was *trying* to work up the courage to ask him if he was in love. Why couldn't she just ask him? Why? It wasn't because she didn't want to know. It was because— Oh, what did it matter? He needed to marry with or without love.

Griffin plucked at his white cuff. "I never said *how* I would go about my courtship, and I certainly never promised to give *you* the details. Or a timeline," he finished with a particularly charming smile.

"Fine. Do you at least intend to ask your future *wife* to dance tonight?" Meredith crossed her arms firmly over her chest. The Southbury Stubborn Streak never stopped her from attempting to convince him to do things *her* way. She could be equally as stubborn if need be.

Griffin tipped his head to the side. "Perhaps."

"I told your mother that you fancy someone," Meredith admitted in a singsong voice.

Griffin shook his head slightly. "Of course you did. Which means you also told her that you have seven guesses. And that you've already used one."

Meredith fingered the diamonds at her neck. "She had some guesses of her own, you know."

"Oh? Do tell," Griffin drawled. He grabbed two champagne flutes from the tray of a passing footman and handed one to Meredith.

"Absolutely not," Meredith replied, taking a sip of champagne. "I'm not about to inform you of who we've discussed. And I'm not about to be hasty about this matter either. It's far too important. I intend to take my time and make a real study of it."

"Do you?" Griffin's voice was entirely nonchalant. Almost *too* nonchalant. Was that a clue?

"Indeed," Meredith replied, watching him carefully lest he give away another potential clue. "I already know she is no one obvious. She couldn't be."

"Why is that?" Griffin took a sip from his flute. More questionable nonchalance.

"Because you are not an obvious man. You're quite nuanced and broody."

Griffin's dark brows snapped together. "Broody? When am I broody?"

Meredith rolled her eyes. "You don't know you're broody? Honestly. With your dark brows and your unfathomable eyes, you can be extremely broody."

"Are my eyes unfathomable?" He laughed and shook his head.

Meredith rocked back and forth on her heels. "Sometimes they are so dark I don't even know what you're thinking." She studied his face. Was he even more handsome than usual tonight? Straight nose, high cheekbones, enviable long, dark lashes. Good God. What was happening to her? Had Clare's words affected her that much? Meredith couldn't possibly be thinking of Griffin...*that* way. It was... Why, it was... indecent.

Griffin took another sip. "I can hardly help the color of my eyes."

"You'll never believe who Clare guessed," she blurted before immediately regretting it. Now *why* had she said that?

He tilted his head to the side again and studied her. "Who?"

"Um...me." She was entirely unable to meet his gaze. She cleared her throat. "Clare said she always thought you and I would end up together." She forced a laugh and shook her head fiercely, still staring out into the crowd. "Of course I told her that was *ludicrous*."

"Ludicrous?" he echoed.

"Yes, yes, of course. Now...does the lady of your choosing have light hair or dark hair?" Meredith continued. Better to focus on the woman he fancied. It kept her thoughts safely off of *his* looks. And his dark, broody eyes, for that matter.

"I never agreed to answer such questions."

"*Humph*. I should have negotiated for them." Meredith scowled and drank more champagne.

"I wouldn't have agreed," Griffin replied. "All I agreed to was to tell you a simple yes or no when you present me with a name."

"Fine. Since I already know it's not Amelia Barnstaple, I'll have to think of someone more likely. It's not Lady Shanna MacGregor, is it?" She glanced at him to see his reaction.

Griffin's dark eyes widened slightly, and, for a heart-stopping moment, Meredith thought she had managed to guess correctly on her second attempt. But then a smile spread over Griffin's lips. "Is that your official guess then?" he asked simply before turning back to survey the crowd.

"Yes." Meredith blew a wisp of hair away from her forehead.

"Then no. It's not her." He sounded far too pleased with himself.

Meredith frowned. "This isn't going to be easy, is it?"

He bit his lip, the picture of innocence. "I certainly hope not."

Meredith narrowed her eyes and contemplated the matter. She'd been considering a variety of names for days now. Amelia Barnstaple had been her first guess because the young woman was sensible, pretty, and clever. She'd been out for several Seasons and was just the sort of unpretentious girl Meredith could picture her friend admiring. She was also precisely the sort of young woman Meredith would like as a friend, and whoever Griffin married would have to be her friend. She couldn't bear it if his bride wanted them to stop being close. But now that Meredith was pressing the issue of his betrothal, she'd begun to think more and more about that sad possibility.

"Lady Catherine Montague?" Meredith blurted.

"No," Griffin replied with a smug smile.

"Blast it." Meredith expelled her breath. But she couldn't explain the relief that swept through her both times he told her she was wrong. What would it feel like when she got it right? What would it feel like to watch Griffin pledge himself to another woman for life? Queasiness settled in her middle.

"That's three guesses. You have four more," Griffin continued, pulling Meredith from her unwanted thoughts.

"I'm well aware of how many guesses I have remaining," Meredith informed him. "You needn't rub it in." She lifted her nose. "Besides, you're not the only one with a secret, you know?" There. Perhaps it wasn't the most subtle way to change the subject, but it would suffice. She wanted to wipe the smug smile off Griffin's face. Just for a moment. And her news was certain to do it.

"I'm not?" Griffin's brows shot up and the point of his tongue came out to barely touch the edge of his mouth.

Her skin heated. Dear God. Why was she noticing things like the location of Griffin's tongue all of a sudden?

"What's your secret?" he drawled, taking another sip of champagne.

Meredith lifted her chin. "Why would I tell you my secret when you refuse to tell me yours?"

Griffin's eyes rolled heavenward. "Because you cannot keep a secret to save your mortal soul, and because you obviously want to tell me or you wouldn't have brought it up."

Meredith frowned. There were times when someone knowing you so well was quite inconvenient. Annoying, really. But Griffin was correct. Ever since she'd talked to Clare and got her much-needed encouragement, Meredith was dying to tell Griff her secret.

"Very well." She moved closer and motioned for him to lean down so she could whisper in his ear.

⁓

MEREDITH'S WORDS were a hot puff at Griffin's neck that made him clench his fist and struggle to remember that she was telling him a secret. "I intend to take a lover."

He *must* have heard her incorrectly. He straightened back up to his full height and stared down at her as if she was a mermaid who had somehow managed to flap herself into a London ballroom. His chest was clenched so tight he couldn't breathe. "You're going to *what?*"

"Shh. Keep your voice down. And I believe you heard me," Meredith replied, taking a small sip from her champagne glass. Her eyes were bright, and a playful smile appeared on her pink lips. Dear God. She was serious, and she was… proud of herself?

"Why this sudden desire to… to…?" He couldn't even say the blasted words.

"Take a lover?" she supplied helpfully.

"Yes." He tugged at his cravat. The damned thing was strangling him.

"What?" She gave him an impish grin. "It's not uncommon for widows to take lovers. I'm hardly an old woman."

"I'm aware," Griffin choked out. Indeed, she was *not* an old woman. She was gorgeous and desirable and her breasts in that gown were driving him slowly mad. But still. Griffin cleared his throat. "Why the sudden desire to…?" No. He could *not* say the words.

"Take a lover?" Meredith repeated, laughing. "I've decided that the two of us are getting quite boring in our old age."

"As you just pointed out, we're hardly in our dotage," he grumbled.

"Precisely," Meredith replied, "but you wouldn't know it by our actions. All we do is sit around the house reading, talking, and drinking tea."

He drew his brows together. "I happen to like reading, talking, and drinking tea."

"I do too, but we're going to waste away there. It's time, Griffin. It's time to live our lives. That's why you shall finally marry, and I shall—"

Griffin closed his eyes. "Don't say it again," he demanded through clenched teeth. He downed the rest of his glass of champagne, took hers, downed the rest of that, and placed both glasses on the tray of another passing footman. "Let's dance."

He didn't wait for her response, only pulled her along behind him toward the floor and swung her into his arms as a waltz began to play.

"My, this news seems to have upset you, Your Grace," Meredith said when they were facing each other again.

A slight growl issued from Griffin's throat. "You know I hate it when you call me that."

"Yes, well. You're a duke and I'm a duchess and we have

become two of the most stuck-in-our-ways people I know," Meredith replied, still grinning.

"There are other ways to find amusement," Griffin shot back.

"Oh? Do tell." Meredith blinked at him. "Whist? Charades? Playing the pianoforte?"

"What's wrong with the pianoforte?" More growling.

"It's boring."

Griffin clenched his jaw. Too many thoughts were roiling through his brain. He didn't know how he was able to speak. Meredith had managed to shock him. Her aversion to marriage was something Griffin had not attempted to talk her out of. Yet. But he'd never guessed she'd say something like... Dear God. *She wanted to take a lover*. Of course unattached women in their circles did such things, but Griffin had never thought for a moment that *Meredith* would. Meredith just seemed so...content with her life as it was.

Ever since Griffin had returned from the war, Meredith had been adamant about never marrying again. She made it a point to say often and loudly that she had "absolutely no desire whatsoever" to tie the parson's noose around her neck again. But a lover? A lover? It was unfathomable. He'd always assumed—perhaps incorrectly—that she'd had an unpleasant time of things with Maxwell when it came to marital relations. Honestly, Griffin hated thinking about it. But now she wanted a lover? Damn it. He was going to have to think about it. Quickly.

"When did you come to this decision?" He was trying his damnedest to keep the anger from sounding in his voice. He had no right to be angry, of course.

"Several weeks ago," Meredith replied, a far-too-bright smile on her face.

"And you didn't tell me?" His frown deepened.

"You didn't tell *me* you had chosen a bride," Meredith pointed out.

She had him there.

Damn. Damn. Damn. This wasn't part of the plan. He'd intended to slowly reveal his feelings to her and then once she was amenable to the idea, he would point out that marriage to him would be far different from marriage to an old man. Then at the Midsummer Night's Ball, he would fall to his knee, declare himself, and she would say yes. Just as she'd always dreamed. Just as *he'd* always dreamed.

Only he'd assumed that he would have time to discuss it with her first. Ensure she was amenable to the idea. He'd thought he'd have all Season, in fact. He had enough patience to wait. But now here she was forcing the issue.

"Do you already"—he had to clear his throat as the damned words were stuck—"have someone in mind?" *Ugh*. The question was bitter on his tongue.

"No," she replied quickly.

A wave of relief sluiced through Griffin's body. "How do you intend to find this man?" he bit out.

Meredith's smile widened. "That's the best part. I told Clare about it, and she told me about a club. A *secret* club where patrons find—*ahem*—interested parties. She says it's a den of iniquity."

Bile rose to the back of Griffin's throat. His eyes narrowed to slits. "What *club?*"

"It's called the Onyx Club."

Damn. Damn. Damn. Blast. Damn. And fuck. How did Clare Handleton know about the Onyx Club? Griffin had never been there. It wasn't his sort of place. But Ash was a frequent patron, and Griffin had heard enough stories to know it was hardly the type of establishment Meredith should visit. Part gaming hell, part pleasure club, it was a location where the *ton*'s most debauched members preferred to spend time. Everyone there wore masks so they wouldn't be recognized, but according to Ash, most were thinly veiled disguises and the people wearing them weren't particularly interested in whether they were identified.

Damn. Damn. Damn again. Griffin's mind raced. He had a problem. A real one. Meredith had already declared that she would never marry, but if she was going to take a lover after all this time, he was going to ensure it was *him*.

CHAPTER EIGHT

Three Nights Later, The Duke of Southbury's Bedchamber

Griffin tugged viciously at the cuff of his white starched shirt. His valet had just finished helping him dress. In addition to the shirt, he wore buff-colored buckskin breeches, a sapphire waistcoat, and a white cravat. A black demi-mask lay on a nearby tabletop.

He stared at his reflection in the cheval glass in his dressing room and scrubbed a hand roughly through his hair. Fuck all. He was really going to do this. He was going to go to the Onyx Club tonight to keep an eye on Meredith.

He'd tried his damnedest the other night to talk her out of it. Tried every day since then too. He'd even begged her to allow him to come along to keep her safe. But she'd refused his every plea. The lady had made up her mind, and tonight was the night.

Of course Meredith going to the club was a horrible idea. He'd tried to explain that to her. But she was too blasted stubborn. Meredith had always been the sort who needed to experience things for herself. You couldn't tell her anything.

Hadn't he tried—no, begged—her not to marry Maxwell? But she hadn't listened then and she wouldn't listen now. Griffin's only choice was to watch her and make sure she didn't get hurt. Ash would expect no less.

Oh, Griffin had toyed with the idea of trying to seduce her himself. After all, it would be an unholy temptation. But that would be wrong. Even if Meredith was looking for an intimate encounter with a stranger, it would be wrong to know who she was and not reveal his identity. But he could go to the club and watch her. Ensure she didn't end up with a scoundrel or, worse, someone who would be rough with her. Hurt her. He clenched his fists. If anyone tried to hurt her, he'd kill the bastard.

Griffin shook his head and sharply sucked air in through his nose. He could only hope that once she arrived at the club, she would quickly realize the error in her judgement. After all, according to Ash, the Onyx Club wasn't for the meek or the faint of heart. The only problem was…Meredith wasn't meek. Far from it, actually. But would she truly go through with something as bold as taking a stranger as a lover?

There was only one way to know for certain.

∽

NOT HALF AN HOUR LATER, Griffin's coach dropped him at the back entrance of the Onyx Club. He'd been forced to do some serious acting when he'd asked Ash for advice on how to conduct himself inside.

Ash nearly had a laughing fit when Griffin informed him that he intended to spend an evening at the Onyx Club. Of course, Griffin had *not* informed the marquess of his own sister's intentions to go there. But after his laughter died down, Ash had realized that Griffin was quite serious.

THE DUCHESS HUNT

Ash told him about the secret entrance at the back of the club, where urchins ran back and forth summoning coaches. According to Ash, for the correct amount of coin tossed their way, they were quite discreet about the patrons' identities. A gentleman's coach carried his family seal, after all.

Mask firmly in place, Griffin entered the stone archway at the rear of the club, gave a pound note to the door attendant, and was shown to a special table in the back where he took a seat. He'd already heard the club rules from Ash. No names. No personal questions. And no sharing any stories about his time at the club. Simple enough.

Griffin ordered a brandy from a footman wearing gold and black livery and turned to watch the crowd. The ladies' attire was a far cry from the demure gowns worn at the *ton* events he was used to. The women here wore gowns pulled down so low their nipples were nearly exposed. Their skirts were cut up to their thighs. Their lips were painted red, and their hair was loosely held up by a few pins.

The men were equally relaxed. No overcoats. Relaxed cravats. Tight breeches that left very little to the imagination. They all wore demi-masks, but already Griffin recognized more than one person here. Thinly disguised, indeed. Ash had been right.

Raucous laughter and curse words flew through the air, while drinking, gambling, and plenty of fondling appeared to be the order of the day. Griffin searched the rowdy crowd, scanning every woman's face for Meredith. He would know her anywhere. Though he couldn't imagine what she might be wearing tonight. To his knowledge, Meredith didn't own anything scandalous enough to wear here. But if Clare Handleton had known enough about this place to recommend it to Meredith, she must have also known enough to tell Meredith to alter her attire for the occasion. And

Meredith herself had already mentioned the masks. She clearly knew that much.

A lady in a bright pink satin gown that revealed *far* too much sidled up to him. "You're new here," she declared with a wide smile, her blue eyes sparkling behind her white silken mask.

Griffin didn't recognize her. "Indeed. Am I so obvious?" he drawled.

"I would have noticed you before, handsome." She reached out and dragged a bare finger along his jaw. Apparently, the women here didn't find gloves to be a necessity either.

Before Griffin had a chance to say more, she plunked herself down on his knee and wrapped her arms around his neck, pressing her generous breasts to his chest. "Care to go upstairs?"

Hmm. Seemed there was little pretense at the Onyx Club. Not that he hadn't expected as much. Griffin was no stranger to the attentions of bawdy women. He'd certainly spent some enjoyable hours with his share of barmaids at school, but this woman's cloying perfume did not tempt him. He stood and helped her to stand, ensuring she was steady on her feet before releasing her elbow. "No, thank you."

"No, thank you?" she echoed in a prim accent before letting out a far-too-loud laugh. "A polite chap, aren't you?"

He narrowed his eyes at her. Was she a well-to-do member of the *ton* looking for amusement, or was she a courtesan? Apparently, both sorts of ladies frequented this establishment.

"Good evening, my lady." He bowed to her, grabbed his drink, and took off into the crowd. The fewer people who laid eyes on him, the better. The last thing he wanted was to cause a scene or to be recognized. But would Meredith recognize him? How could she not? Which is why he didn't intend to introduce himself to her. He would simply find her and keep an eye on her. From afar. Perhaps dissuade an overly amorous suitor from making her an indecent proposal if he had to.

Griffin took a stroll around the perimeter of the place. His walk revealed several more people he knew—or thought he did. Many of the men were married. Not shocking, but Griffin couldn't help but think that once he managed to convince Meredith to marry him, he would never stray from her side.

After completing his perusal, Griffin decided to take up residence near the front entrance. He hadn't seen Meredith in the crowd, and he guessed she'd enter through the front of the establishment as most ladies did.

He leaned against the wall near a faro table, close enough to watch the play as if he was interested, but far enough away to be clear he wasn't interested in participating. The better part of an hour passed, and he'd been forced to decline the advances of three more women before the black curtains at the front of the establishment parted and Meredith stepped inside.

He knew her immediately. After all, he'd memorized everything about her. He'd know her full pink lips and the delicious curve of her shoulders anywhere. Her luscious dark hair was captured in an unruly bun at the nape of her long neck. Her glowing gray eyes peeped out from beneath a jade-green demi-mask.

Apparently, her friend *had* told her about the dress code because tonight Meredith was wearing a dress unlike any he'd ever seen her in. It was made of jade-green satin with matching tulle wrapped around the shockingly low bodice and a tight satin skirt that was cut up to her thigh. When his gaze traced the creamy curve of her long leg up to where the slit stopped, Griffin had to swallow. Hard.

Damn it. She couldn't be here dressed that way. She'd be approached by half a score of men in mere moments.

Behind her mask, her alert eyes darted through the crowd. Her eyes were the only part of her that belied a certain hesitancy, a bit of anxiety. But soon, after she'd taken in the scene in front of her, she squared her shoulders and began to walk determinedly toward the nearest bar top.

Griffin watched her from beneath his lashes, still feigning interest in the faro game. He mustn't follow her too closely or she might see him and recognize him.

She slid onto one of the black wooden stools in front of the bar and spoke quickly to the barkeep. Griffin was too far away to hear what she said above the din. The barkeep left and returned a few minutes later with a glass of dark liquid in a snifter. Griffin raised his brows. Meredith was obviously drinking real alcohol tonight. No simple glass of champagne for her. Which meant he'd have to watch her even more closely. She was rubbish when she drank too much, and more than two glasses of champagne was too much for Meredith.

Not moments after the barkeep walked away, pocketing the coin Meredith handed him, another man appeared at her side. This man wore tight breeches, a purple waistcoat, and a leering smile. His dark-blond hair was slicked back and— Dear God. Was that the Earl of Marsden? He was married and a total lecher. Surely, Meredith would recognize him and send him away.

The earl pulled his stool so close to Meredith's that he was breathing down her neck. And taking in an indecently close view of her *décolletage*. Griffin clenched his fist. His fingers ached to punch the man in the throat and toss him across the room.

THE DUCHESS HUNT

When the earl reached out and traced Meredith's collarbone with a gloveless fingertip, Griffin had to close his eyes and count to three to keep himself from stalking over there and ripping the earl off the stool.

But Meredith leaned back, and the earl's hand dropped away from her. Good. Marsden had just been saved from bodily harm...for the moment.

Griffin narrowed his eyes at the couple. Meredith was imbibing far too quickly, which meant she was nervous. It wasn't long before her glass was empty, and the earl flagged down the barkeep to order her another.

Griffin continued to watch them. She accepted the new glass with shaking hands. The earl reached out to touch Meredith's cheek. That was it. Whether she knew it was him or not, Griffin *had* to send Marsden packing. Griffin pushed himself off the wall and stalked toward the couple, intent on upending Marsden's barstool for a start. But just as the earl's hand nearly reached her, Meredith's arm shot up, and she blocked his touch. Then she swiveled quickly on her seat. Her eyes swiftly searched the crowd, and her gaze locked directly on Griffin's. He was standing midway between her and the wall, but his eyes were intent on her. She hopped off her seat, tossed a few words to Marsden, and made her way unerringly toward Griffin.

Damn. She knew him. She must have recognized him. Why else would she be heading straight for him? But it didn't matter. She was clearly trying to get away from Marsden's unwanted attention, and Griffin was ready to help. She would ask him what he was doing here, and he would simply tell her the truth. He sucked in a deep breath, ready to plead his case.

Meredith came to a stop in front of him. "Sir, will you please pretend you're talking to me?"

Griffin blinked. "Pardon." It was an idiotic thing to say,

but it had simply fallen from his lips. Did she not realize it was him? Truly?

"Will you pretend to know me?" she asked more frantically this time, glancing back towards Marsden, who had stood and paid and was on his way toward them.

Now was not the time for confessions. "Yes, of course," Griffin quickly amended.

"Thank you," she whispered. "A gentleman at the bar was overly friendly, and I'd like to excuse myself from his company. With your help, if you don't mind."

"Do you know who he is?" Griffin asked.

Her brow crumpled into a frown. "I thought we weren't allowed to ask personal questions or discuss names here."

Griffin shook his head. What had he been thinking? "Yes. Of course. Regardless, I'm happy to help you."

They didn't have time to say more because Marsden arrived, his leer firmly in place. "My lady. Off so soon? I thought we were having an interesting conversation," he said in a wheedling tone that made Griffin want to punch him even more.

"Seems the lady prefers *my* company," Griffin said, giving the arse a tight smile.

"But *we* had just begun *our* acquaintance," Marsden said while staring directly at Meredith's breasts.

Griffin's knuckles cracked as he made a fist. It would feel so good to punch this bastard in the face.

"I was interested in continuing my conversation with the lady here," Marsden continued.

"And she's *not* interested in continuing it," Griffin shot back, his eyes narrowing on the earl.

Marsden lifted his nose in the air. "I should like to hear that from the lady herself, if you—"

"He's right," Meredith said, raising her chin and forcing

Marsden's gaze to meet hers. "I am *not* interested in continuing our acquaintance...Sir."

"Ah, but I had just purchased your drink," Marsden said, his smile downright unctuous.

Griffin's knuckles cracked again. What sort of man, let alone a purported gentleman, would mention the fact that he purchased a lady's drink...as if she owed him anything in return?

Griffin pulled a coin from his coat pocket and flipped it to Marsden. "There's your money. Now be off with you."

Meredith smiled behind her glass.

Marsden grabbed the coin and pocketed it, his own smile still tight. "It's not about the coin, Sir," he said in a mock-offended voice. "I had hoped—"

"We all know what you had hoped. Now leave or I'm happy to continue this conversation with you alone...in the back alley." It took everything in Griffin to keep from telling Marsden to go home to his long-suffering wife. But no names, he reminded himself. And no personal information.

The earl's eyes narrowed to slits, but after a few moments, he turned abruptly on his heel and left.

"Thank you," Meredith said, breathing a long sigh of relief after Marsden melted into the crowd.

Griffin bowed. "You're quite welcome, my lady."

"How do you know I'm a lady?" Her eyes were filled with suspicion and perhaps a hint of...alarm?

"Merely a guess," he reassured her, shrugging. She still didn't recognize him. Interesting. Well, it was dark in here and she had been drinking and...this was the last place she would expect to find him, even though he *had* offered to come with her.

She was taking too large sips of her drink. She had to be intoxicated. The encounter with Marsden had obviously shaken her.

"Why are you here?" he blurted.

She turned her head to the side and eyed him carefully. "That isn't a personal question, is it?"

He allowed the hint of a grin to touch his lips. "I hope not because I'd very much like to hear the answer."

She took another quick sip of her drink. "What if I don't want to tell?"

He nodded. "That is your prerogative, of course."

"Why are *you* here?" she countered. Another sip.

He expelled a breath before deciding upon his answer. "I am checking on a friend."

She lifted a brow. "A lady friend?"

He tipped his head from side to side. "Perhaps."

She eyed him carefully. "So you're *not* looking for an… arrangement?" Was that disappointment in her eyes?

"An arrangement?" he echoed.

She shook her head, and her gaze dropped to the floor. "My apologies. This is my first time here. I'm not certain precisely what you call it."

"Would you believe it's my first time here too?" he answered quietly.

Her head shot up and surprise registered in her eyes. "Truly?"

"Yes. This isn't my usual sort of…" He glanced around and shrugged again. "Crowd."

She nodded slowly and took a long sip from her glass. "I wasn't certain what to expect."

"And? How do you find it now that you're here?"

She rocked back and forth on her heels. Such a Meredith thing to do. "A bit intimidating, if I'm honest. But…" She stopped, lifted her chin, and looked him square in the eye. "I must say *you're* quite handsome."

Griffin nearly choked. "Par…pardon?"

She bit her lip. "I'm sorry. Is that too forward? I was

under the impression that being forward is how things are done here." She drained her glass.

Griffin scrubbed a hand through his hair. Damn. He was acting a complete fool. But he'd never expected to encounter her this way, speak to her like this. And he should have taken that blasted glass out of her hand when he'd had the chance.

She held up her empty glass. "Will you…buy me another?"

"Don't you think you've had enough?" He nearly rolled his eyes at himself. He was hardly acting the role of the intrigued suitor. But something told him not to blurt out his identity quite yet. Perhaps it was the way she was looking at him. Perhaps it was the way she'd told him he was handsome. Perhaps it was the desire to keep her from slapping him and stomping off to talk to another man, which she might well do if he told her who he was right now.

"Funny. The man in the purple waistcoat was only too eager to buy me a drink," she replied.

"The man in the purple waistcoat was trying to take advantage of you."

She giggled. *Giggled*. Meredith never giggled. Confirmed. She was drunk as a wheelbarrow. "And what if I *want* to be taken advantage of?"

Griffin had no time to respond to *that* leading question before Meredith's arms were around his neck.

Time stopped. Griffin had dreamed of this moment for years. Hell, there had been nights sleeping on a cot in the army where this exact same development had played out in his imagination time and again. But in every single one of the fantasies, Meredith knew who he was. Knew who he was and wanted *him*. That was his dream. Not this.

He made to pull her arms from around his neck, but she plastered her body against his and said, "Take me somewhere where we can be alone."

Griffin's body betrayed him by going rock hard. He swore

under his breath, clenched his jaw, and *forced* himself to say, "You've had a lot to drink."

"Or not *nearly* enough." Meredith lifted on her tiptoes and kissed him.

CHAPTER NINE

Meredith couldn't believe her luck. She'd nearly lost her nerve and abandoned her plan to come here tonight at least half a dozen times. But each time she'd told herself she was being a ninny. And she reminded herself of why she was doing this. She wanted to live. She wanted to have fun. She wanted to experience passion with a young, handsome, virile man and—well, for now, passion would do. And it turned out brandy was absolutely lovely. It was making the room spin a bit, but it was also making everything seem like a lark. It was ever so exciting here. Especially with *this* particular man.

She'd finally made it to the club wearing the scandalous gown she'd had commissioned just for tonight. She'd had the buttons placed on the sides so she could dress and undress herself. Ingenious, if you asked her. And Madame Bonary had been only too eager to help. She'd paid the modiste a hefty sum, but it had been worth it. The jade gown was absolutely perfect. When she'd first put it on, her maid's eyes nearly popped from her skull. Meredith had sworn the young lady to secrecy. And she'd been nothing but thankful for the matching feathered satin mask that she'd commissioned along with it. Who knew that wearing a mask could make you feel so free? And so scandalous?

She'd hired a hack to bring her to the club. Then, after paying a pound, hearing the rules, and being ushered inside past the swinging golden lanterns and black curtains, she'd nearly cast up her accounts at the first look at the place. Her nerves had scattered through her belly. Had coming here been a mistake?

The Onyx Club was quite a sight. Crowded, loud, and filled with people who were obviously much more experienced than she. She was far, far out of her element. But she was too frightened to turn and run. Too frightened or too stubborn. She wasn't quite certain which any longer. And so, the only alternative had been to put one foot in front of the other and move farther into the large, intimidating space.

She'd begun at the bar top. As good a place as any. A drink would help calm her nerves, she'd reasoned. And she'd ordered brandy. Champagne seemed far too mild for a place like this. Not five minutes had passed before the man in a purple waistcoat came over and whispered something positively indecent in her ear. She should have been flattered. She should have been glad to have found someone who appeared to be interested so quickly, but that man, whoever he was, had been too brash, too eager. She didn't like the feral look in his eyes or the way he leered at her and stared only at her breasts. No doubt she was terribly naïve, but she wanted someone who would move a bit slower. Give her time to think.

Thank heavens for this man, Mr. Sapphire Waistcoat. He'd been calmly propped against the far wall, looking like a beacon in a storm when she'd first spotted him. Then, when she'd needed a place to run to, he'd been there, even closer than before. And when she'd got up very close to him, she realized that he was excessively handsome. He smelled good, a familiar scent that made her feel safe. In fact, he reminded her a great deal of…Griffin. He seemed kind like Griffin too. He certainly wasn't trying to pressure her into doing anything. On the contrary, he'd just mentioned that she'd had too much to drink. Which was true. But this was what she'd come here for, wasn't it? To find a handsome man and…well, go somewhere private with him. The drinks had emboldened her enough to ask. There were private rooms upstairs. Or so Clare had been told.

Now that she had her lips on Mr. Sapphire, she didn't regret it. Because his hot mouth opened and slanted across hers, and he pulled her body against his as his tongue tangled with hers. It was as if she went up in smoke, mind and body. *Young, handsome, and virile, indeed*. She'd never experienced anything like it. Unfortunately, it was far too brief because nearly as quickly as he'd transformed the kiss into something mind-numbingly intense, he pulled her hands from around his neck and stepped back.

"No." He shook his head.

"No?" she echoed, feeling bereft. "What do you mean no?"

"I mean you're not in a state to make a decision like this."

She leaned toward him and gave him a saucy half-smile. "I made the decision before I walked in the door tonight."

That kiss had certainly made her feel as if he wanted her. So why was he telling her she wasn't in a state to make a decision like this?

"Be that as it may," he said.

"My friend, Griff—" She stopped and shook her head. *No names*. "I have a friend who often says that."

The man froze. His shoulders didn't move, and his breathing stopped.

Something triggered her memory. Was it his voice? The way he stood? He *did* remind her of Griffin. "In fact," she continued, peering at him more closely, "you look quite a lot like my friend." And he really did. Tall, muscled, dark hair, dark eyes. He looked *very much* like Griffin. But it couldn't be Griffin. Could it? Ooh, why did the thought thrill her a bit? She eyed him carefully. "If I didn't know any better, I would think you *are* my friend." She forced a laugh. "Only he would *never* be at a club like this." Hadn't he spent the last few days trying to talk her *out* of coming here?

No. No. This wasn't Griffin. That made no sense. Perhaps she was more inebriated than she thought.

Mr. Sapphire closed his eyes. "I don't think—"

No. No thinking. Not tonight. She wanted someone who was equally uninterested in thinking. The room was spinning faster now. She wanted this man. Besides, Griffin was positively delicious, so why *wouldn't* she want someone who looked like him? Did it matter if she'd be thinking of Griffin while they—?

No. No. No. That *had* to be the drink talking. She didn't fancy Griffin in that way.

Did she?

Hmm. He *was* quite fine to look upon and his body was— Oh, why couldn't she banish thoughts of Griffin? And this man *definitely* wasn't Griffin. *He couldn't be.*

"Are you going to take me to a room, or do I need to seek my pleasure elsewhere, sir?" Oh my. Had those words truly come out of *her* mouth? That had been forward, hadn't it? She would never say such a thing if she weren't half-sauced and wearing a mask.

Mr. Sapphire's jaw clenched. He groaned. Perhaps she'd been a bit heavy-handed in demanding his answer, but his putting her off had bruised her feelings. Was she not pretty enough? Not desirable enough? The thought caused the old pain to slice through her. Her husband rejecting her. Sending her away. Blaming her.

THE DUCHESS HUNT

No. None of that tonight. This was the place where men and women came to engage in scandalous pursuits, was it not? If this man wasn't interested, then she would just have to find a man who was.

He huffed a deep breath before grabbing her hand and pulling her behind him. "Come with me."

Meredith smiled to herself. Ooh, good. She'd won.

∼

TUGGING MEREDITH BEHIND HIM, Griffin stalked over to the bar and asked the barkeep for a key. Thank God Ash had told him how it all worked before he'd stepped foot in this place. Griffin hadn't been planning to get a room himself, of course, but Ash had shared the information just the same. Now it was proving useful.

Damn Meredith and her stubbornness. In the scant moments Griffin had had to contemplate the matter, he'd decided the safest course would be to take her to a room where they could be alone. She needed to sober up. And he needed time to think. No doubt he would have to come clean, take off his mask, and admit to following her here, but first things first. He couldn't allow her to drunkenly trip about the club looking for just anyone to take her upstairs. The next man she ran into was likely to have the scruples of the Earl of Marsden or worse. And that would be a disaster.

After securing the key to room seven, Griffin led Meredith behind him through the black curtains at the back of the room, down a short corridor, and up a staircase to the second floor. They moved through the hallway together, not saying a word until they came to the room. He unlocked the door and allowed her to precede him inside.

Griffin remained in the hallway for a few moments, trying his damnedest to sort through his thoughts. That kiss had been scorching. As if it had changed the alchemy of his soul. Feeling Meredith's mouth on his, her lips, her tongue, her body sliding against his, had been seconds of pure torture. It hadn't been a choice, really, to lean into that kiss, to pull her fully against him.

Thank God he'd come to his senses quickly enough to put an end to it. Or he could have taken her right there against the wall near the faro table. That's not what she wanted. At least it wouldn't be when she was clearheaded.

But she *wasn't* clearheaded. Which had to be why she hadn't recognized him. He'd done nothing to disguise his voice. Was a mask truly that concealing?

She'd said her friend would *never* come to a place like this.

Think again, Mere. I wouldn't come to a place like this unless you *were here*.

There was only one proper way to handle this. Let the drink wear off and tell her the truth. He would pray later that she would listen to him and just go home. She had to.

Griffin took another deep breath. Then he pushed open the door and stepped into the dimly lit room. The flash of a flint lit up the space for a moment before a lantern's soft glow replaced it, and when his eyes finally adjusted, Griffin realized that Meredith was standing in front of him in nothing but a flimsy shift.

CHAPTER TEN

"Jesus Christ." Griffin's breath left his body in a rush.

A huge smile spread across Meredith's face. "So, you *do* think I'm pretty?"

His eyes devoured her. No harm in telling the truth. "Pretty? You're beyond pretty. You're the most beautiful woman I've ever seen."

She laughed. "Well, that must be an exaggeration, especially given the fact that you cannot see my face, but it makes me feel good, so thank you."

"It's not an exaggeration. I don't need to see your face." *That* was certainly true.

But when she began to slowly pull one strap of her chemise from her shoulder, Griffin closed his eyes. "Please don't."

Meredith's words were slightly slurred. "What ss-sort of man are you?" She pointed a wobbly finger at him. "You kissed me downstairs, and you just told me I'm the most beautiful woman you've ever ss-seen. But you don't want to look while I remove my chemise? I don't understand. Did I misread your intentions?" she finished, letting the strap fall back into place, a confused look on her flushed face.

Griffin's forehead beaded with sweat. His jaw was tightly clenched. Of course she didn't understand, but now was not the time to reveal himself. He sensed it would only anger her. "If you take off your shift, I may not be able to stop myself," he said instead. *Also, true.*

A smile spread across her face. "Well, that's a relief." She moved toward him and lifted herself on tiptoes to whisper in his ear. "I believe being unable to stop yourself is the entire point, sir."

He shook his head. "You don't understand. I…"

She dropped back to the balls of her feet and frowned. "You what? Do you like me or don't you?" She pushed out her lower lip in a pout.

Griffin blew out a long breath. This was excruciating. "I… I can't in good conscience make love to a woman who is inebriated."

"Are you quite serious?" she asked with a sharp laugh. She flung an arm toward the door. "Half the couples downstairs ss-seem to be inebriated to me. In fact, I'm not entirely certain I could do this if I were ss-sober-minded."

"Be that as it— I mean, *regardless*, I wouldn't want you to regret it come morning."

Meredith stood staring at him with her hands on her hips. "You're ss-serious, aren't you?"

"Quite." He nodded.

She blinked and frowned. Taking a wobbly step backward, she braced her hand against the wall, obviously to steady herself. "Well, how do you like that? I have ss-somehow managed to find the one ss-scrupulous man in a den of iniquity." She laughed a humorless laugh before she turned toward the chair in the corner where she'd tossed her gown. She grabbed it, clearly intending to put it back on.

"Do you plan to find someone else then?" Griffin asked from behind her. Damn. Damn. Damn. Should he reveal himself? Or would that only anger her?

She turned to face him, the gown still clutched in her hands. "That depends." She lifted her chin.

"On what?" His throat worked as he swallowed.

She tilted her head to the side for a few seconds, obviously contemplating the matter. "On whether you *will* accommodate me if I am not inebriated next time."

Beneath the mask, his eyes widened. "Next time?" Oh, God. Was there to be a next time?

"Yes. I'm not certain what you're interested in, but I am interested in an agreement. An arrangement of ss-sorts. One in which a man of my choosing and I meet regularly. Temporarily, of course."

"I see," he said, frantically trying to decide his next move.

"If you're interested in the ss-same and we find we are compatible—*ahem*—in bed, I will go home tonight and come back to meet you another time."

He nodded eagerly. Perfect. She would go home tonight, and he would have time to think about how to handle her *next time*. Perhaps, as her friend, he could talk her out of coming back here. "Yes. I'd like that."

Griffin nearly slid to the floor with relief. For more than one reason. First, it meant that she would be safe tonight, and second, he would be spared from the unholy temptation of touching her again.

Meredith's eyes narrowed to slits. "On *one* condition."

Warning bells sounded in his brain. "What's that?"

"That you'll kiss me again before I go."

Damn.

CHAPTER ELEVEN

By God. Griffin honestly didn't know if he could. Kiss her again and stop, that is. Holy Christ, seeing her in her shift was nearly killing him. Her body so lithe and graceful. Her skin like silk. Her breasts nearly visible beneath the delicate lace of the shift. He was barely able to breathe, let alone think. Kissing her again might send him to his grave, but if that was her condition to leave here tonight without going any further, then so be it.

He let out a deep, shaky breath and stepped toward her. She lifted her face to his. The masks covered their cheeks, their eyes, and their foreheads, but their lips were free. Free to do this.

Griffin slowly lowered his mouth to hers and touched her lips so gently he barely felt it. The moan deep in her throat made his cock ache, and his arm snaked around her waist to pull her tight against his rock-hard body. His mouth shaped her lips and gently, slowly, coaxed them open. When they did, his tongue slid inside her wet warmth. She moaned again and Griffin closed his eyes. The satin of their masks rubbed together, and then the kiss exploded. Her tongue moved to tangle with his and her arms moved up his chest to wrap fiercely around his neck. Before he even knew what he was doing, he had walked her backward to the bed and lowered himself atop her. Her shift had pushed up to her hips and her right leg snaked around his calf to hold his body against hers. His hips moved of their own accord. He pressed against her intimately, nudging again and again against the softness between her legs. The sounds of pleasure she was making in response to his thrusts were driving him wild.

"Yes, please," she moaned. Then she grabbed one of his hands and moved it down to her nearly bare hip. "Touch me," she begged.

He should stop. But he couldn't. His hand moved along the silky skin of her hip, along her thigh, and came to rest between the juncture of her legs. "I shouldn't—"

"Touch me," she begged. "Please. I need you."

He closed his eyes and moved his fingers to slowly stroke her tender, wet flesh. She was ready for him. She wanted him. It would be so easy to undo his breeches and bury himself inside her. But he couldn't do that. He wouldn't do that to any drunken woman. And certainly never Meredith. But he could give her some of what she wanted tonight. He could make her feel good.

His fingertip found the little nub hidden between the folds of her sex. He found it and carefully stroked it once, twice.

Her head pushed back against the mattress, and she moaned deep in her throat, exposing her neck to him. "God, yes," she breathed.

Griffin clenched his jaw. Sweat beaded on his brow. This was going to kill him, but now he desperately wanted to give Meredith what she'd come here for. Pleasure. Intense pleasure. All of it.

He stroked her again and then settled his fingertip into

place, drawing tiny little circles against her swollen nub. Her leg tensed against his calf and her eyes rolled back. A look of pure ecstasy was pinned to her face. Her breathing hitched with every stroke and her arm was locked tight around his neck.

He wanted to kiss her everywhere, to rub his heavy, needy cock against her, but he was mesmerized by the look on her face. Meredith taking her pleasure. He'd imagined this a thousand times before, but it was more glorious than anything he'd ever conjured in his dreams.

Her breathing came in short pants and her leg trembled with tension as he kept up the gentle pressure. Round and round and round went his fingertip. Then he slowly moved his hand down to slip a single finger inside her.

"Yes," she cried against his mouth, arching her back.

Griffin closed his eyes and swallowed hard. She was so wet, so ready. His finger found the rough spot on the inside of her slick inner wall that he knew would drive her wild. He quirked his fingertip, pressing against the spot. Just enough pressure to—

"Oh, God. Oh, God. Oh, God." Meredith clutched at his arm and her cries of pleasure reverberated through his body, centering on his swollen cock. Each breath, each moan, made him harder. And even though he hadn't had his own release, a pleasure like he'd never known spread through his body.

Meredith was sobbing into his ear. Her body was shaking. Tremors echoed through her. He'd just given her a climax. A climax that had made her scream and clutch his shoulders while her body quaked beneath his. He smiled to himself.

Breathing heavily, he pulled himself away from her and stood, not trusting himself unless he put space between them immediately. He spent several seconds staring down at the floor, willing his cockstand to subside while he concentrated on setting his breathing to rights.

A few moments later, Meredith shifted on the bed, and he turned back to look at her. Her face was filled with…astonishment?

"That was…" Her voice was shaking. Her eyes were wide. "I've never felt anything like that."

Griffin frowned. He wasn't surprised, but he hated to hear it. "I hope you don't regret that in the morning," he said, giving voice to his greatest fear.

She shifted to sit up and patted the space beside her on the bed. He stepped back and lowered himself to sit next to her. She pushed herself up to her knees, gently turned his chin toward her face, and kissed him softly. "I will never regret that. There's not enough brandy in this world." She gave him a sexy smile. "Thank you."

Griffin remained motionless on the bed while Meredith spent the next several moments pulling on her gown and buttoning it. When she was dressed again, she turned to him and winked. "Until next time, Mr. Sapphire. Next Thursday night?"

Words failed him. All Griffin could do was nod.

He watched her go, a hundred thoughts racing through his head. What the hell had he done? There was no coming back from this. What could he possibly do next time? If he revealed his identity, he would risk angering Meredith so much she might never speak to him again. If he didn't reveal himself, she would expect them to go further. To make love. If he didn't come back to the club, she might find another man. Another man like Marsden. Or worse.

Damn it all to hell. This was an untenable situation. He never should have come here in the first place. He never should have got involved. Meredith was a grown woman. Where she went and what she did and with whom weren't his business. Fine. His heart might shatter if she took a lover, but that didn't give him the right to do what he'd done.

Damn it. He'd had a plan. Court her. Woo her. Make her fall in love with him. Give her the dream of her first Season. And when she was ready, when she'd finally come to realize that they were the perfect match for each other, drop to one knee and propose to her at the Midsummer Night's ball. But none of it was going according to plan.

Griffin scrubbed a hand through his hair again, cursing himself for being seven times a fool. How in the hell would he *ever* make this right?

CHAPTER TWELVE

The Next Morning, The Duchess of Maxwell's Bedchamber

Meredith groaned and rolled over as her maid pulled open the heavy drapes that covered the windows. She squinted and pressed her fingertips to her temples. Ugh. She was more than a bit under the weather. Which stood to reason. She'd downed two brandies in the space of an hour at the Onyx Club last night. Good heavens, what had she been thinking?

She rubbed her forehead. The truth was she *hadn't* been thinking. She'd been frightened and nervous and drank too much as a result. Mr. Sapphire had been right when he'd said she'd had too much to drink. But then he'd gone and made love to her anyway. Apparently, he hadn't been able to stop himself. And she didn't regret it. Not one bit. When he'd pressed his hips to hers again and again, it had been a completely different feeling from what she'd shared with Maxwell.

Last night she'd felt wetness between her legs and desire, real desire. As if she couldn't get enough of the stranger in blue. And then when he'd touched her like that... Well, Maxwell had never done *anything* like it. She'd been telling the truth when she'd told the stranger that she would never regret it. She already wanted to do it again.

It had been the most erotic night of her life. The feel of his hard shoulders beneath her fingertips, his lips on her neck. And when he'd touched the bare skin of her thigh, she'd thought she would go up in smoke. After that, his touch. Between her legs. She shuddered. She'd had no idea her body was capable of such ecstasy. It was exactly what she'd wanted when she'd decided to take a lover. Unparalleled pleasure with a man who knew *exactly* what he was doing.

Meredith smiled to herself again. She may have been foxed, but she had enjoyed every single moment of her time in that room with Mr. Sapphire, and she was certain she would enjoy it even more when she met him next time. Seeing him again, touching him again, was nearly all she could think about.

She bit her lip. There was only one thing that troubled her about last night. Each time Mr. Sapphire had touched her, Griffin's face had appeared in her mind. She knew why, of course. Mr. Sapphire was quite like him. His height. His body. His eye color. His hair color. They could be brothers.

She shook her head. Oh, what did it matter? She couldn't —no, *wouldn't*—ever have a relationship like that with *Griffin*. Did it matter if the man she chose to pleasure her looked like him? She obviously had a sort that she found attractive, and Griffin's physical characteristics were that sort. That wasn't anything to be ashamed of. It was perfectly natural to be attracted to tall, dark, and handsome men with muscles for days. And if one of them had fingers that could drive you wild with passion, all the better.

But...they *did* look quite alike...

Only Griffin wouldn't be at the club. Griffin wouldn't—

Meredith shot straight up in bed, clutching the sheet to her chest as panic spread through her limbs. Wait a moment. Griffin wouldn't be at the club *unless* he'd gone there to follow her!

The memory of how she'd met him last night played through her mind. She'd sought *him* out. He'd been there. Close by. Watching her. She'd asked him to help her, and he'd seemed so familiar.

Her mouth dropped open with wonder as the impact of her thoughts fully settled into her pounding head. Suddenly, it all made sense. The warnings he'd given her about drinking too much, his mentioning that it was the first time he'd been there too, the way his voice and scent had triggered her memory. If she hadn't had two brandies, she would have known immediately.

She'd gone to bed with Griffin last night!

She sat in silence for several moments as the thought filtered through her mind. Then, a small smile curled her lips, and an unexpected thrill shot through her. *She'd gone to bed with Griffin last night.*

No wonder he'd put off her attempts at going further at first. But then he'd— Another shudder went through her at the memory of his touch. *Thrilling.* Now it made sense that he'd shut his eyes and said, "Please don't…" when she'd begun to remove her shift. He'd gone on to say that if she did so, he wouldn't be able to stop himself. It wasn't that he didn't want her. He'd been trying to wait until she was sober-minded, until she knew it was him.

Which meant…he'd wanted her too!

Because she didn't have one moment's doubt that, all along, Griffin had known it was her.

And oh, my God, what exactly did *that* mean?

CHAPTER THIRTEEN

The Next Evening, The Harrisons' Ballroom

"Meredith, there you are," came Gemma's bright voice from several paces away.

Meredith turned to see the debutante and her older brother headed her way through the crowded ballroom. Oh, God. Was she blushing? She never blushed.

The pair came to a stop in front of her.

"It's good to see you, Gemma, Southbury." Meredith kept her gaze trained on Gemma. She could not look at Griffin. *Could not.*

"Good evening, Meredith," Griffin said as he bowed over her hand, the picture of propriety as usual.

Meredith glanced away when he straightened. Oh, God. She couldn't look Griffin in the eye. He obviously didn't have the same problem. *Why didn't he have the same problem?* How could he act as if he hadn't been at the Onyx Club? As if she hadn't been crying into his ear with pleasure?

Meredith cleared her throat and shook her head. She

needed to say something. She was acting strangely. Being far too quiet. "Are you enjoying the party?" she said, more to Gemma than Griffin.

"I *was*," Gemma replied, a frown on her face.

"Oh, dear, what happened?" Meredith asked, still steadfastly diverting her eyes from Griffin. She tugged at the bodice of her gown. Why was it so hot in here tonight?

"Lady Mary Costner is at it again." Gemma sighed.

Meredith played with her necklace next. Anything to distract herself from thoughts of being in bed with Griffin at the club.

"What did Lady Mary do this time?" Meredith was desperately trying to feign interest in Gemma's words, but all she could think about were Griffin's hands on her body, making her explode into a thousand pieces, making her moan and—

"She is positively horrid," Gemma continued. Her hands had turned into fists on her hips and a mulish expression covered the younger woman's face. "You should hear the things she said to poor Cecily tonight."

"Who?" Meredith asked. Was she *perspiring*? Honestly. She dabbed at her forehead.

"Cecily Grundy?" Gemma answered.

Ah, yes, Cecily. Excellent. Something to concentrate on other than Griffin's hands and mouth and— Meredith cleared her throat. She moved her gaze over to the larger-than-usual group of wallflowers. Cecily Grundy was a plump girl with an unfortunately abrasive and overbearing family. But she had always been a sweet soul with blazing orange hair, cornflower-blue eyes, and a bright smile on her face. Cecily waved at Meredith, who waved back before turning again to Gemma. "What did Mary say?"

"I hate to repeat it," Gemma said, shuddering. "But mostly

she made light of the fact that Cecily hasn't been asked to dance since the Season began. Poor Cecily was nearly in tears."

"Oh, dear. That does sound awful," Meredith agreed, wincing.

"Why does Lady Mary even care?" Gemma continued. "She's already made it quite clear that she has set her sights on the Duke of Grovemont. He's the most eligible man in the room. Besides Griffin, that is," Gemma finished with a smile aimed at her brother.

Griffin arched a brow in response. "Don't drag me into this. I have no intention of offering for Lady Mary."

"I'm certainly glad to hear *that*," Gemma replied, still smiling.

"Excuse me for a moment, won't you?" Griffin asked.

"Go, go," Gemma said, waving him away.

Meredith let out her pent-up breath. She'd been only too happy to excuse him. She shook her head again and tried to recenter her thoughts on what Gemma had been saying. Meredith frowned. Wait. "Is it true? Cecily hasn't been asked to dance *all* Season?"

"Yes," Gemma replied solemnly, nodding. "I'm afraid so. I've asked half a score of gentlemen to ask her to dance, but not one of them said yes."

"Oh, dear," Meredith replied.

Gemma crossed her arms over her chest and huffed. "There are times when the snobbery of the *ton* makes me want to scream. It's positively unfair how a lady must be possessed of beauty, money, *and* a good family if she is to have any hope of finding a decent match."

"I agree with you," Meredith replied as she contemplated the situation. Cecily was the youngest daughter of a bankrupted baron. She wore clothes that weren't particularly fashionable. She giggled far too much when she was nervous, and she had an unfortunate tendency to tell rambling stories. But every young lady deserved to be asked to dance. At least once. Meredith tapped a finger to her lips. "We must see to it that she is asked to dance and by someone who—"

"Wait a moment!" came Gemma's surprised voice.

Meredith glanced up and followed Gemma's gaze to the dancefloor, where, to her delighted surprise, she spotted Cecily twirling about in the arms of none other than…Griffin. Cecily was staring up at him as if he were Adonis descended from the heavens. Griffin was looking down at the girl as if she were the only woman in the room.

Meredith's heart clenched. Griffin was the kindest soul she'd ever known. Oh, why hadn't she thought to ask him to begin with? She could only blame it on how befuddled she'd been in his company tonight. Of course he was dancing with Cecily. Of course he was.

Meredith watched with a bright smile on her face and a sheen of tears in her eyes as the waltz ended and Griffin escorted Cecily back to her mother and sisters' sides. He made small talk with the family and gave Cecily a deep, formal bow over her gloved hand before leaving them and returning to where Meredith stood.

"Are you quite all right, Mere?" he asked when he was again by her side. Gemma had flown off somewhere, no doubt to help the next wallflower in need.

"Yes," Meredith breathed. She wanted to give him a big hug. She *would have* given him a big hug if it was at all suitable to hug a man in a ballroom. "That was one of the loveliest things I've ever seen you do. And I've seen you do many lovely things."

"It was my pleasure," Griffin replied with a wink. "She's a sweet girl."

Oh, no. No more blushing. Meredith pressed her palms to her cheeks and the two of them watched as a small line of gentlemen formed next to Cecily's mother, clearly vying for the opportunity to ask the girl to dance.

As the next gentleman took Cecily out on the floor, she caught Meredith's gaze, and a huge smile lit up her face. "Thank you," she mouthed. Meredith realized that Cecily believed *she* had been responsible for sending Griffin over. She nodded and smiled in response. She'd tell her the truth later, but for now, Cecily should just enjoy all the dancing.

"Our Society is so predictable," Meredith said with a lighthearted sigh, giving Griffin a sly smile. "A handsome, eligible duke asks a girl to dance and suddenly she's the most sought-after girl in the room."

"You think I'm handsome?" Griffin replied, batting his eyelashes.

Meredith's mouth went dry. The memory of him kissing her neck nearly made her knees go weak. What exactly was his plan? Did he truly intend to act as if they hadn't done what they did? On the other hand, they had both been wearing masks and neither had admitted they'd known the other. Perhaps it was best if they kept up the ruse.

"You know you're handsome, Griff," she finally replied. "Your future bride is going to be quite fortunate indeed." She cleared her throat. Yes. Good. In addition to pretending as if she had no idea it was him, she should continue to keep his future wife in mind each time she thought about kissing him again. "And speaking of your future bride, aside from Cecily, I haven't seen you dance with anyone else tonight." There. Best to change the subject. It might just serve to help her *stop* thinking of him touching her every time she glanced at him.

"Just because you haven't seen it doesn't mean it didn't happen," Griffin replied with that sly smile of his.

Meredith crossed her arms over her chest and arched a brow at him. "So, you've danced with her?"

"No. But I believe you are attempting to keep the subject off yourself, *Your Grace*."

"Me?" She gave him a beatific smile. "Whatever do you mean?"

Griffin lowered his voice. "I mean you went to the Onyx Club, did you not? I've been waiting all evening to hear how it went."

CHAPTER FOURTEEN

Griffin eyed Meredith intently as a shy smile spread across her beautiful face. Was she blushing? Meredith didn't blush.

She lifted her nose in the air. "One shouldn't kiss and tell, *Your Grace*."

"Then one shouldn't inform one's friend one is going to a pleasure club," he easily replied.

Griffin had had all day to think about whether he should ask about her night at the club. He'd finally decided he had no choice. Meredith would find it suspect if he *didn't* ask about it. He'd brought it up often enough earlier this week when he'd tried to convince her not to go. And it might make him horrid, but the truth was, he *wanted* to hear what she had to say about her time in room seven.

Meredith tugged at the end of her glove. "You'll be pleased to know that I was quite safe there."

"Were you?" Griffin arched a brow. She was *definitely* blushing. Hmm. That was interesting. Although knowing what she'd done last night certainly explained why she might blush.

"Yes. Well, *after* I dispatched one particularly unwelcome patron it was safe," she added.

"And?" Griffin prodded.

Meredith bit her lip and glanced at him from the corner of her eye. "And I had a bit too much to drink."

"And?"

"And I found someone quite…"

His brows shot up. "Quite what?"

"Quite agreeable," she murmured.

Oh, she was definitely blushing. "Agreeable?" He narrowed his eyes on her.

"Yes."

Why wasn't she meeting his eyes?

"He's tall and dark and oh-so-handsome. He also seemed quite kind. A real gentleman. And—"

"Handsome, you say? How handsome?" Griffin watched her carefully.

Her throat worked in a swallow, but a sly smile popped to her lips. "Handsome enough that I allowed him to kiss me."

That was interesting. She'd kissed *him,* of course, but he couldn't correct her. "And…?" He cleared his throat, letting his words drift off significantly.

"And it was *quite* enjoyable." She cleared her throat.

"So he kissed you? Is that all?" This was excruciating, but if he hadn't been there last night, he'd be asking these questions.

"Not quite." More blushing.

His brows inched higher. "Did you—?"

She slapped at his shoulder. "Honestly, Griffin. I cannot tell you *everything*."

He blinked at her innocently. "Fine. Then just tell me this. Did you…enjoy yourself?"

Her smile was wicked. "Suffice it to say, I am going back Thursday. To see him again. If he decides to return, that is."

Griffin narrowed his eyes on her. "Why wouldn't he return?"

She shrugged. "How do I know that he enjoyed himself as much as I did?"

"I'm certain he—" No. Better to let that comment go. Instead, Griffin inclined his head. "So, the pleasure club was all you hoped it would be?"

"And more," she breathed.

Damn. There was no doubt he was going to hell for doing this. Here she was telling him about what she'd done with the gentleman she'd met, and Griffin had not only kissed her and touched her, but he still wasn't telling her it was *him*.

What the hell would happen when she discovered he'd lied to her? This entire charade could *not* end well. There was no possible way it could. Griffin had been up most of the night trying to think of an efficient way to end it all. But by the time the sun had come up, he still had no good plan.

To make matters worse, even though he'd told himself a hundred times that he shouldn't, he *knew* he would return to the club on Thursday. What choice did he have? It was wrong, but he couldn't leave Meredith there alone. Marsden and his ilk would be only too happy to swoop in if he wasn't there.

He'd briefly considered taking Ash's advice and telling her immediately that he loved her. But that idea didn't sit well with him either. He still wanted to provide her with the perfect Season, the perfect courtship, the perfect betrothal. She deserved that. Not to mention the fact that he hadn't yet had time to woo her. She might not even say yes if he declared himself so soon. He couldn't risk losing her friendship if the time was not yet right. Damn. Damn. Damn.

"Enough about me," Meredith continued, snapping him from his thoughts. "*You* need to begin courting the woman you're going to marry. An engagement won't just happen without some effort on your part, you know." She glanced around the ballroom. "So…where is she?"

Griffin smiled and shook his head. "That wasn't even a good try. I believe you're on your fourth guess."

Frowning, Meredith pressed her fists to her hips. "How am I supposed to make a proper guess when you refuse to show interest in any lady?"

He bit his lip. "What if I told you I've already shown plenty of interest in this particular lady?"

Her eyes lit up. "Ooh, a clue? How sporting of you, Griff." Meredith tapped her chin with her gloved finger and frowned again. "But I can't think of anyone…except…" This time her eyes went wide and so did her mouth. "*Cecily Grundy?*"

"No," he said simply, staring straight ahead with his hands folded behind his back.

"Oh, you infuriating man! You gave me that clue, knowing I would guess Cecily, didn't you?"

"You cannot prove it." He grinned at her. "That only leaves three guesses, Mere. You may want to be more cautious in future."

"I intend to be, don't you worry," Meredith grumbled. "Now, allow me to give you some advice. You cannot expect to court a lady unless you do things like bring her flowers and take her riding in the park. Have you done *either* of those things?"

"Not yet, but I intend to do both…quite soon."

CHAPTER FIFTEEN

Thursday Night, The Onyx Club

"Looking fer some fun, lovey?" a blond woman in a scarlet-colored gown and matching mask asked Meredith. She was sitting at the bar waiting for Griffin to arrive. The woman had just materialized at her side.

Meredith had thought about it quite a lot, and she'd already decided she would *not* tell Griffin she knew it was him. Because for all she knew, it *wasn't* him. After all, he hadn't taken off his mask. He hadn't admitted it. He certainly hadn't acted any differently toward her at the Harrisons' ball. She'd begun to wonder if she'd been imagining the entire resemblance.

On the other hand, what if it *was* him? What would he say to her tonight? Would he admit his identity? Honestly, it was fascinating to consider. No doubt he wanted to tell her the truth. She guessed he hadn't told her last time because she'd been drunk and kissing him. If it truly was him, she could only imagine his guilt.

THE DUCHESS HUNT

The truth was that she hoped he would not admit his identity tonight. First, there were no names here at the club. That was a rule for a reason.

But there was another reason she didn't want him to admit who he was, a reason she would only admit to herself. A reason that had come to her in the dead of night and shocked her with both its intensity and its veracity.

If Griffin admitted who he was, or if she admitted she knew it was him, she couldn't kiss him again. Because kissing him again—doing anything scandalous with him again—under any other pretext than pretending they were strangers would be wrong.

He was her friend, and she was supposed to be helping him find a *wife*, for heaven's sake. And the truth was...she *desperately* wanted to kiss him again. Perhaps more importantly, she wanted to find out if he wanted to kiss *her* again.

So, no, the man she was set to meet tonight was *not* Griffin. He could not be Griffin because she couldn't go upstairs with Griffin, and she definitely wanted to go upstairs again. If not-Griffin attempted to tell her the truth, she would have to stop him. Thankfully, the club rules were just the excuse she needed.

"I'm...meeting someone," Meredith replied to the blond woman who was still indolently watching her. She tried not to stare, but the woman had on more powder and rouge than Meredith had ever seen. Was she a harlot? Oh, she had so many questions for her, but none of them were probably appropriate to ask.

"I've got somethin' fer ye. If ye're interested." The lady's light brows waggled.

Meredith cleared her throat. She'd read of things like *ménage à trois* and no doubt this was the sort of place where one could partake in such goings on, but how exactly could Meredith make it clear she wasn't interested? She didn't want to hurt this woman's feelings. "I... I don't think so." There. Would that suffice?

"Ah, but ye 'aven't even seen wot I got ta offer."

To Meredith's surprise, the woman pulled a short stack of cards from her bodice. She splayed them out on the top of the bar.

"It's a card game," the woman explained. "Erotic cards, that is. For ye and yer lover, when 'e arrives, per'aps?"

Erotic? Meredith glanced at the cards. They were covered with images of men and women in different stages of undress. "Oh," she murmured, leaning down to take a closer look. *That* was interesting.

The woman bent over and whispered into Meredith's ear. By the time the lady had finished detailing precisely how the card game worked, Meredith was quite interested indeed. In fact, it sounded like *just* the game to play with Griffin— No! *Not* Griffin. *Mr. Sapphire.* That was his name. That's what she would call him. Much easier to pretend that way.

If he arrived.

"Two quid," the woman offered, eyeing Meredith up and down. "Cuz ye look like ye can afford it, me lady."

Meredith didn't deny it. She quickly fished in her reticule and pulled out the money. She slid it across the bar top to the woman.

"'ave fun, lovey," the woman said with a wink before dropping the money into her bodice and disappearing into the crowd.

Meredith gathered the cards and hid them in her own bodice. A small smile popped to her lips as she downed the rest of her glass of champagne. She'd just purchased a scandalous deck of cards. And she had every intention of playing them with a man she was almost certain was *her best friend.* What *else* would she do tonight? With her not-so-mysterious lover? Honestly, she couldn't wait to find out.

She shook out her shoulders as a slow burn made its way through her body. She'd spent a considerable amount of time fantasizing about tonight. Which was why she was only drinking champagne this evening. She didn't want Griff—Mr. Sapphire!—to accuse her of being inebriated. Not tonight. Tonight, she wanted him to kiss her again, touch her again. The cards couldn't hurt either.

When the barkeep came around, she declined a second glass of champagne. Instead, she watched with interest as the masked ladies all around her flirted shamelessly with their gentlemen. She spied them carefully, determined to learn a few things.

Another quarter hour passed before she allowed her gaze to scour the darkened club again. She'd yet to see her Mr. Sapphire, and with each passing moment, she feared that he'd decided against meeting her again. Perhaps that was Griffin's plan so that he would not have to reveal himself. If he never returned, he would never have to confess. But that also meant that he didn't want her as much as she wanted him. Had he only gone along with everything last time because she'd been foxed? The thought made her frown. She drummed her fingertips against the bar top. Was this madness? Should she just go home?

Probably.

Perhaps she should have one more glass of champagne. What would it matter if he wasn't coming? She was about to flag down the barkeep when she felt it. An internal jolt, a sense, a *knowing*. He was here.

She sat up straight and glanced toward the back of the room just as he stepped through the black curtains. He was wearing his black mask and another dark-blue waistcoat. Her breath caught in her throat. He was so handsome. More handsome than she even remembered. And yes, he was Griffin. She was certain of it now. How could she ever have *not* known? His firm jawline. His broad shoulders. The way he carried himself. *Griffin*. She made a mental note to be more careful with brandy in future.

He had been searching the crowd, and when she glanced at him again, it only took moments for their gazes to lock. He inclined his head in greeting before making his way unerringly toward her.

When he reached her side, he bowed. "Good evening, my lady." His deep voice went straight to her core. She shifted on her seat.

His familiar scent, like pine and the ocean, wafted over her. She must have been frightened and inebriated indeed to have not recognized him last time. She wanted to put her arms around his neck and her nose to the crook and breathe him in.

"I'd begun to worry you wouldn't come back," she replied, drawing her fingertip along the edge of her bodice to draw his attention to her breasts. The other women here tonight seemed to do that often. An excellent idea.

His eyes were immediately drawn to the spot she'd hoped. Then he eyed her up and down. Tonight she was wearing a ruby-colored gown that was every bit as revealing as the one she'd worn last time. His dark eyes flared. He obviously liked it.

"Never think it," he replied. "But there's something I must tell you."

"Let's go upstairs first." No doubt that had sounded particularly forward, but Meredith was *dedicated* to being forward tonight. And she had no intention of listening to his confession if, indeed, that was his intent. Behind these masks, they could be anyone they wanted to be. They weren't Meredith and Griffin, friends with a complicated history and no business kissing. They were simply two people who wanted each other. They could pretend and *keep* pretending. And that's precisely what Meredith wanted.

Fortunately, he didn't argue. She watched him hungrily as he ordered two glasses of champagne and requested the key to a room just like last time.

Then they silently made their way upstairs together. When they stopped at the door to the room, Meredith lifted her brows. "Room seven again?"

"It's a lucky number, is it not?" he drawled.

"I hope so," she said, lowering her lashes over her eyes and then glancing up at him in the same coquettish way she'd seen the ladies do downstairs.

He unlocked the door and ushered her inside.

The moment the door closed behind them, Meredith turned to him in a swirl of red skirts. "Care to play?"

She had no intention of allowing him to speak first. If he told her the truth tonight, he would ruin everything. And she deserved this. This night. One more night of pleasure with no strings attached. What did it matter that Griffin was the one behind the mask? She wanted him. She guessed he wanted her. There was plenty of time to go back to their duchess-hunting tomorrow. Oh, she had a tug of guilt for whoever the lady was that Griffin had already decided to marry. But he had yet to begin his courtship. He'd told her as much. And what his future duchess didn't know wouldn't hurt her. Besides, Meredith would put an end to this before he actually became betrothed. Of course she would.

One of his dark brows had shot up. "Play what?"

She slowly pulled the deck of cards from her indecently low bodice. "A card game. I'm told it's quite diverting."

His eyes sparkled beneath his obsidian mask. "What is the game?"

"The club had these cards specially made," Meredith continued, repeating what the woman downstairs had told her. "Each card has one item of clothing for a man and a woman listed on it. You must remove the item on the card when you draw it."

His mouth quirked. "How does one win the game?"

"The winner is the one with the most clothes left when the cards run out."

"Are you certain that's not the loser?" He laughed. A deep throaty laugh that made Meredith rub her thighs together in anticipation. She wanted him again. Tonight. And if she played this card game correctly, they would end up naked together in bed. A thrill shot through her.

She tipped the flute to her lips, set it down, and then took a seat on the bed. He moved over and placed his drink next to hers. She was trying to shuffle the deck when his gaze locked on hers, and his large hand covered her small one. He took the cards from her and the deck came to life within his fingers. He quickly shuffled them a half dozen ways. The cards flew through the air between his palms, making a whirring noise. Griffin always had been an expert at shuffling cards. She should have realized long before now he was good with his hands. She bit her lip. Oh, *what* a wicked thought.

He offered her the deck again. "Before we play, there's something I must—"

"No," Meredith insisted, still intent on keeping up their ruse. "You sound far too serious. Let's play first." She pulled the cards from his hands and set the deck atop the quilt. "Ladies first?"

He nodded. Thank God. He hadn't insisted. Which meant he wanted this too. She shuddered with relief as she turned over the first card.

The card contained five words: *hair pins or top hat.*

She pushed herself up on her knees and slowly moved her hands to the back of her neck. One by one, she pulled out her hairpins.

His eyes danced with dark fire as he watched the mass of her thick hair fall below her shoulders. She shook it out.

"You're gorgeous," he whispered.

"Thank you," she replied. His words reminded her of when he'd said she was the most beautiful woman he'd ever seen last time. Had he meant that? Had he truly meant it?

She lowered herself back to the mattress and pointed to the cards. "Your turn."

He took a deep breath and flipped over the next card. *Gloves or cravat.*

"Seeing as I'm not wearing any gloves, I suppose the cravat must go," he drawled.

Meredith watched in fascination as his deft fingers moved up to his neck. With one swift tug, he had the cravat undone. Then he easily unwound it and tossed it aside. His shirt fell open, exposing a muscled chest with a light dusting of dark hair. She licked her lips.

He splayed his hand toward the deck. "My lady."

Squirming with anticipation, Meredith moved her fingers to the cards and flipped the next one. *Slippers or boots.*

She daintily lifted her legs in the air and kicked off first one slipper, then the other.

"I'll remove my boots too," he offered, shucking them. "Which means it's your turn again."

She flipped another card onto the smaller stack. *Shift or drawers.* "Oh, my."

His brow quirked. "That means…"

"That means I must take off my gown too, I suppose." A shiver went through her.

"That means I win?" he breathed.

"And I win too." She was already off the bed and plucking at the buttons at the side of her gown.

"Wait." He stood beside her, his hand on hers, stilling her.

She frowned. "Why?"

"We played our game, but I still need to tell you something first. It's important."

No. No. No. *No*. She couldn't allow that to happen. "I don't want to hear any confessions."

"I must tell you who I am."

"Absolutely not!" Her voice was forceful. She lifted her face to his. "You're breaking the rules." *Thank God for the rules.*

He traced the line of her throat with one fingertip and the hint of a smile touched his lips. "Aren't rules made to be broken, sweetheart?"

She swallowed. She just wanted him to keep touching her like that. To keep his mask on. To keep pretending… "I don't want to know who you are," she whispered brokenly. *Because then I can pretend you're not Griffin.*

His hand stopped.

"I don't *want* you to know who I am," he continued. "But I *must* tell you."

"No." She shook her head hard. "No, you mustn't. In fact, you're *not allowed* to. Club rules."

"I cannot in good conscience—"

"If you tell, you'll have to leave the club. Is that what you want?" Instead of saying more, she quickly removed her gown. Then, equally quickly, she pulled the chemise over her head and tossed it atop the small table. She stood there in only her stockings. She was naked. That *had* to shut him up.

He sucked in his breath. "Oh, *that's* not fair."

She stepped toward him and wrapped her arms around his neck, breathing in his maddening scent. "No more talking. Just touch me."

Without another word, his mouth moved inexorably down to meet hers.

For Griffin, it was as if his body was not his own. He needed to put an end to this. He needed to stop it. Immediately. But he couldn't seem to keep his hands off her. If only she hadn't taken off that damn gown and then that even *more damned* shift. She was nude, for the love of God. Naked save for her stockings. Was there a man alive who could resist that? The woman of his dreams standing in front of him without a stitch of clothing, begging him to make love to her?

God damn it. He must have done something truly awful in his life to deserve this torture.

But one kiss wouldn't hurt. Would it?

The moment their lips met, Griffin knew he was lost. Her arms locked around his neck and she clung to him, making tiny whimpering noises in the back of her throat, which made his cock instantly hard. Just one kiss would not be enough.

And what a kiss; it was explosive. His tongue tangled with hers. His hands moved down to cup her backside and suddenly he found himself picking her up and laying her on the bed. He hovered over her, his arms braced against the mattress on either side of her shoulders. She was busily unbuttoning his waistcoat. Mindlessly, he allowed her to. She didn't want to know his name. She'd made that clear enough. But she did want to touch him. Perhaps he could allow her to do that too. Before it went too far. Just for a moment... or two.

His waistcoat and shirt were soon gone and then her frantic hands were working at the buttons at the fall of his breeches. He grabbed her hands then, first one and then the other. Grabbed them and pinned them to the mattress above her head using only one of his hands.

"Let me touch you," she breathed.

He moved his mouth to her neck and devoured her sweet skin. "I can't. We can't—"

"You promised that we would. Oh, God!"

His other hand had dropped below her waist and his finger had found her sweet spot, found it and then moved even lower to slip inside.

He closed his eyes. "You're so wet. So wet and so hot."

"I want you," she breathed against his cheek. "Please."

"I can't." He gently kissed her temple. "Believe me when I say I want to, but I *can't*."

∽

HIS FINGER MOVED inside her then and Meredith forgot the question, forgot all words, as stars exploded behind her eyelids. Her hips moved with his hand, helpless against anything other than trying to find that sweet relief. His fingers were in charge now. Not thought. Not logic. Not anything but the maddening feeling of bliss building between her legs. She wanted her release, and she wanted him to give it to her.

He began kissing down her body, lingering at her breasts, pulling her nipples into his hot mouth, first one and then the next. She sobbed in the back of her throat as he gently tugged the swollen points with this teeth. Then his head moved lower, down, down between her legs. His soft hair brushed against her thighs, and then the smooth slide of his mask near her most intimate spot. And when his tongue flicked out to lick her tight nub, she cried out and filtered her fingers through his hair.

Oh, God. What is he doing? And please don't ever let him stop.

She wanted to reach for him, to touch him between his legs, but he captured her wrists once more.

"Please, let me feel you," she begged.

He shook his head between her legs, saying no, tantalizing her more as his tongue kept up its gentle assault in the spot where she most needed it. He lapped at her, while her knees closed tightly against his shoulders and her body trembled. And when the last licks sent her hurtling over the edge to oblivion, she called out.

A name.

One man's name flew from her lips as waves of pleasure cascaded through her body.

Meredith laid there silently for several seconds as the pleasure receded. When her limbs finally stopped shaking, she realized what she'd done…and whose name had been on her lips when she found her pleasure. And she realized that it could ruin everything. She had to fix it. Quickly.

"Oh, my God. I didn't. I mean—"

He didn't say anything, just stood and quickly pulled on his shirt. He didn't even bother to shrug on his waistcoat. Instead, he grabbed the rest of his clothing and lunged for the door.

He remained silent as the door swung closed behind him.

CHAPTER SIXTEEN

The Next Day, Hyde Park

Griffin stirred his mount alongside Meredith's as they galloped along the dusty path near the water's edge. Her cheeks were rosy, and she was laughing. God, she was beautiful when she laughed.

Today she was wearing a light-blue riding habit and a matching bonnet with black boots and white kid gloves. She was buttoned up to the neck and covered down to the ankle. But Griffin couldn't keep from remembering the last time he'd seen her. Her gorgeous body laid bare beneath him, taking her pleasure.

Saying his name.

When he'd arrived at her town house this morning, it had taken nearly everything in him not to fall to one knee and declare himself. To put an end to their pointless guessing game by admitting his feelings for her. But after what had happened at the club last night, how could he? Instead of admitting his identity last night as he'd intended, he'd touched her... More, he'd given her pleasure with his mouth.

THE DUCHESS HUNT

So intimate. Which made him *not* telling her worse. *Much worse*.

But there was something else. He'd got the distinct impression last night that she'd *known* it was him. Something about the way she kept insisting he not tell her who he was. Something in the way she looked at him, touched him. Their gazes had locked and, somehow, he'd just felt that she knew him. Only he'd been too uncertain to ask. And she'd obviously wanted it that way as well.

There could be only one reason she didn't want to admit it. Because she didn't want it to be true. She didn't want it to be *him* touching her. She wanted it to be a stranger. A man she had no connection with. If she returned his feelings, she would have admitted she knew him. And that thought devastated him.

But saying his name had to mean something. Didn't it? That she wanted *him*, that she was thinking of *him* when she'd found her release. But if that was the case, why hadn't she allowed him to tell her the truth? Why hadn't she admitted that she knew him? It made no sense.

Damn it. He should have revealed his identity immediately. She might have said she didn't want to hear it, but surely it would have been the right thing to rip off the mask and show his face *after* she'd said *his bloody name*. Only he'd made *another* mistake. He'd grabbed his things and run away like a fool. Blast. Blast. Blast. When had everything become so complicated?

Right about the time you decided to put on a mask and follow Meredith to a pleasure club.

He glanced over at her, laughing in the sunlight. In addition to asking her to go riding in the park today, he'd brought her flowers this morning. And not just any flowers. Lilies, her favorites. Didn't she realize he was attempting to court *her*? If so, she gave no indication, acting the same as she always did when they were together. But she had to know. Which was more proof that she didn't want to admit it. Didn't want it to be true. Didn't want him. Not as a husband.

She only had three more guesses. Would she guess correctly, or would he finally be forced to tell her? At this point, Griffin *wanted* her to guess herself. It would be nothing but a relief. Damn it. Perhaps Ash was right. Perhaps Griffin should just say it, tell her, forget the plan and consequences be damned.

"When was the last time we went riding in the park?" Meredith asked, shaking Griffin from his torturous thoughts.

He watched her from the corner of his eye as she slowed her horse to a canter. If she was at all affected by what had happened last night at the club, she was doing an excellent job of hiding it. She hadn't acted a bit differently toward him today. Meanwhile, Griffin felt as if his world had been picked up and dumped upside down.

"It's been too long," he replied, slowing his horse as well. He had to remain as nonchalant as she was. That was the only way to get through this outing.

"Far too long," Meredith agreed. "We should do it more often."

She stopped and dismounted.

"Agreed." Griffin stopped and dismounted too.

He tied both horses to a nearby tree trunk before making his way to Meredith's side. They walked together through the soft green grass toward the water's edge. Meredith took a seat atop a large boulder nearby, and Griffin lowered himself to sit next to her.

He braced a palm on his knee. "How did it go last night? At the Onyx Club?" He had to know her thoughts. She couldn't possibly be as unaffected as she seemed. He also wanted to see if she gave anything away that proved she knew it was him.

THE DUCHESS HUNT

Meredith tucked a stray bit of hair beneath her bonnet. "It, er… I'd rather not talk about it, actually." She gave him a shaky smile and didn't meet his gaze.

Hmm. So she *was* affected by it? Good. He wasn't the only one. But *did she know it was him*? He still couldn't tell. She might simply be reticent to share such intimate details with him.

She was facing the water, and he watched her profile. Was Meredith…blushing again? Was she remembering how she'd said *his* name last night? Jesus Christ. This ruse was untenable.

"Things didn't go badly, did they?" he prodded. Because if he hadn't been there himself, *that* was the next question he would ask.

"Not…exactly." She shrugged one shoulder in that familiar way of hers and the hint of a wicked smile touched her lips. "He…wanted to tell me his name. I did *not* want that."

Griffin sucked in his breath. His chin dipped. There was his answer. She couldn't be any more clear. She knew it was him, and she was telling him in no uncertain terms that they should continue to pretend their time at the club was disguised.

"I had…quite a lot of fun," she continued.

He lifted his head. "Fun? Is that what you call it?" God damn it. He was *in love* with her. Didn't she know it? Or didn't she care? She was obviously attracted to him at least. There was no way she was faking her reactions in bed with him. She'd enjoyed herself. She'd just admitted it. But what did that mean? She didn't want a future with him…only pleasure? Is that why she hadn't allowed him to tell her who he was last night?

Meredith expelled her breath, stood, and smoothed a gloved hand down the front of her riding habit. "I've been thinking a lot, Griffin, and I..." She glanced away, almost nervously.

What was this? Meredith was never shy. Had he mistaken things? Was she about to tell him? Was she about to recount what had happened last night? Admit she knew it was him? His breath caught. His heart hammered.

"I'm ready to make my next guess about the identity of your future bride," she finished.

Griffin expelled his breath and shook his head. *That* had been the last thing he'd expected her to say. "Intent upon changing the subject, I see." He couldn't help the frustration in his voice. Because he already knew she would never guess herself. She didn't want to know the truth.

She didn't respond. Fine. He'd prodded her enough. She had the right to change the subject. "Go ahead then. Guess." He reached down and grabbed a stone from the grass beside the boulder.

"Miss Caroline Bounty," came Meredith's voice, but she hardly sounded convinced.

Griffin drew back his arm and threw the stone. It skipped across the water. Jesus. This was more excruciating with each passing moment. He wanted to pick up the goddamn boulder and throw it into the lake. "I'm afraid not."

Meredith heaved a sigh. "Fine. And don't say it. I know. Only *two* guesses left. I'll have you know, I'm running out of ideas. I like Caroline very much. She would make a fine wife. And I could have sworn you were looking at her at the ball the other night."

Griffin frowned. "Was Caroline there?"

Meredith threw up her hands. "Oh, you're impossible." She took a seat on the boulder again.

"So I've heard," he replied with a halfhearted grin. Hefting another stone in his hand, Griffin glanced over at Meredith. "May I ask you a question?"

"Of course." She turned to face him and perched her folded hands atop her knee. "As long as it's not about what I did last night."

"It's not." He shook his head. God damn him to hell. He already knew what she did last night. No. Today he wanted to know *why* she was so intent on his marriage. Why she couldn't bloody well admit she had feelings for him. Feelings that *he knew* were far from *friendly*.

She nodded. "Very well. Ask then."

"Why is it you don't give your brother the same hell you give me?"

A wistful smile appeared on Meredith's lips. "About getting married, you mean?"

"That's precisely what I mean. He's an unmarried marquess. He needs an heir too. Why are you so set on pairing *me* off?" He tried to keep the irritation from his voice, but he hadn't been entirely successful.

Meredith smoothed her skirts over her knee and shrugged again. "You know Ash. He's hopeless. Trying to convince him of anything is like talking to a stone wall. He says he'll never marry. I suspect he will, but not a day sooner than when he's good and ready."

Griffin settled his shoulders and lobbed another stone across the water. "And I'm what? More…pliable?" So much for nonchalance.

She stood and stared off across the water. "Ha. You've never been pliable, Griff. But you are more *reasonable*. At least you admit you'd like to marry and that you should. You've given every indication that you intend to settle down. You simply need a bit of a push."

Griffin stood and smiled wryly. "I should count myself fortunate then to have such a dear *friend* to push me."

Meredith leaned down and plucked a daffodil from the ground near the boulder. "You know you need to marry,

Griffin." Her voice took on a serious tone. "You may not have wanted it, but you're the duke now. Your mother—"

"I'm well aware of my mother's feelings on the subject," Griffin ground out. "Don't you think *your* mother would want Ash to marry too?" Why was he bringing this up? Because it kept the focus off himself.

Meredith bit her lip and frowned. "I suppose if Mama was still alive, she would push Ash to marry. I think he's convinced he'll end up like Father."

Griffin arched one brow. "A horse's ass, you mean?"

Meredith shook her head. "No. Alone." A frown line appeared on her forehead. "Father did the best he could."

Griffin's jaw clenched. He'd heard this argument time and again from Meredith. It always angered him. "Your father went to London and left the two of you to fend for yourselves before returning only when you were ready to make your debut and forcing you into the first match that came along. An awful match at that."

Meredith's jaw was tight. She shook her head determinedly. "No. He picked Maxwell. He chose a *duke* for me. Mama wanted that." Her voice was low and heated.

"A duke at any cost?" Griffin shot back, his hands on his hips.

"What do you mean by that?" Her voice trembled with anger.

"You know what I mean, Meredith. The cost of your happiness."

She folded her arms over her chest and drew up her shoulders. "I had to marry someone."

Griffin expelled his breath. He glared down at the grass beneath his boots and lowered his head. "I've always thought you could do better. Find love."

She slashed an arm through the air. "Perhaps. But if I'd

married for love, you and I might not be as close as we are. Have you ever thought of that?"

"Every damn day." Griffin clenched his jaw. They'd had this discussion time and time again. It never ended in a satisfying way. The fact was that he'd begged Meredith not to marry Maxwell all those years ago. His pleas had fallen on deaf ears. Then and now.

He lifted his head and shook it.

"No good can come from us rehashing the past this way," she said quietly. "What's done is done."

Oh, yes, time to change the subject as it always was when things got too intense.

Griffin grabbed up another stone and tossed it in the air. Pretending to be nonchalant was going to bloody well kill him. "Are you worried that Ash will marry someone you don't like?" he asked, doing his best to infuse the conversation with their normal lighthearted tone once more.

"Not at all." Meredith's answer had been too quick. She was clearly still shaken too.

"Why?"

The hint of a smile touched her lips. "Because by the time Ash marries, I shall be far too old to care." Ah, there she was. The Meredith she wanted everyone to see. The one who was never hurt, never angry. Quick with a jest. The eternal *friend*.

The woman who refused to see what she clearly didn't want to see.

Griffin forced a half-hearted smile to his lips. He was playing with fire now, but perhaps fire was needed. "Ash told me if I tell the woman I fancy that I fancy her, he will choose a bride next Season."

Meredith's jaw dropped open. Her eyes went wide. "Are you jesting?"

"No." He shook his head. "Can you believe it?"

Meredith stepped toward him and put a hand on his

shoulder. He wanted to turn his head and graze her hand with his cheek. He wanted to close his eyes and feel her soft skin against his. Instead, he kept his gaze locked on hers.

∽

"I wouldn't pay much mind to what Ash says about marriage," Meredith replied with a breezy little laugh, patting Griffin's shoulder.

She was doing her utmost to feign nonchalance because her skin had gone clammy. Her heart thundered in her chest. The deeper they'd got into this conversation, the more uncomfortable she'd felt. Because it wasn't just him following her to the club. It wasn't just him not telling her who he was before he'd made love to her. Now she realized that she was the woman Griffin had been talking about when he'd said he already knew who he would marry. He was talking about *her*. He wanted to marry *her*.

She'd swallowed a sob that had risen in her throat.

She couldn't let him say it. She couldn't. Because that would make it real, and she would have to refuse him. And then their friendship would never be the same. And her heart would shatter.

Griffin couldn't marry her. He had to marry someone who could give him an heir.

"If I tell her how I feel," Griffin continued, "I would deprive you of your final guesses."

Meredith pulled her hand away, turned, and closed her eyes. This was excruciating. "Yes, you wouldn't want to do that."

"I also admit I worry she may not return my feelings." His voice was filled with emotion. It made Meredith's heart ache.

She forced a cheerful smile to her lips and turned back to face him. "If she doesn't, there are plenty of other ladies—"

"No," Griffin breathed. "There is no other lady for me."

Meredith held her breath. Oh, God. Oh, God. Oh, God. This was too much. They needed to leave. Go back home. Pretend none of these words had ever been said.

"Do you remember what you told me that Clare said to you during your last visit?" Griffin asked, tossing a small stone in the air and catching it.

Of course she did. She'd told him that Clare thought *they* would end up together. Meredith had said it as if it were the most ludicrous notion in the world—she'd even used the word "ludicrous"—but she'd said it.

Meredith frowned. She had to play dumb. There was no other way out of this. "What Clare said?" She tapped her jaw with her gloved finger. "Wait a moment. Do you mean—?" Her eyes went wide.

"Yes?" he prompted, searching her face.

She cupped a hand over her mouth and did her best to feign surprise. "I can't believe I didn't see it. The answer has been right under my nose this entire time. Could it be?"

He wiped the back of his hand across his brow. "Say it," he murmured.

"Clare!" Meredith said it in the most unassuming manner she could. Of course she didn't believe for one moment it was Clare, but she had to say something to keep him from naming her. Because she couldn't allow him to say it aloud and change everything. She just couldn't.

Griffin closed his eyes briefly. "Clare?" He shook his head. "No. Not Clare."

Meredith let her face fall as if disappointed in her incorrect guess.

∼

"No more guesses today," Griffin snapped.

Meredith was obviously pretending, but he wasn't about to force her to name herself. It had all happened too fast, been too soon. He wouldn't push any more today.

"Very well." Meredith smoothed her skirts, obviously happy to change the subject again. She expelled a long, deep breath. "Let's discuss Gemma's prospects then, shall we?"

Griffin's shoulders relaxed. An excellent idea. Gemma *was* a much less frustrating subject. "I saw Gemma dancing with Lord Driscoll the other night. She seemed to be enjoying herself."

Meredith shrugged. "I thought so too, but according to Gemma, he was far too loud."

Griffin furrowed his brow. "Loud?"

Meredith nodded. "Afraid so."

"I don't blame her then. Loud doesn't sound pleasant at all."

"I agree." Meredith sighed. "And spending her time chasing the debutantes out of the corners at parties is not helping Gemma make her own match. So, with your mother's blessing, I've decided to host a dinner party for her. I intend to invite the most eligible bachelors. Though it's too bad Grovemont can't attend."

"What's the matter with Grovemont?" Griffin asked, frowning.

"Apparently, he's left town to tend to his mother. She's taken quite ill, from what I understand."

"I'm sorry to hear that." Grovemont was a good man and a good friend. He was Griffin's age, so perhaps a bit old for Gemma, but she could certainly do far worse.

"Perhaps it's for the best," Meredith replied. "Besides you, Grovemont is the most eligible bachelor of the Season, and according to Gemma, Lady Mary Costner has staked her claim on him."

Griffin winced. He didn't envy Grovemont at the moment. "Does Grovemont return Lady Mary's affections?"

Meredith rolled her eyes. "For his sake, I hope not. She sounds like a monster."

"Well, with or without Grovemont, a dinner party for Gemma is an excellent idea. Thank you."

"Good. I'm glad you agree. I shall plan it for early next week. Now, we should probably be going."

Meredith looked relieved when Griffin took her elbow and led her back to where the horses were tied.

After helping her up, he boosted himself back into his saddle. "Tell me. Do you plan to return to the Onyx Club?"

This was it. An unspoken challenge. Last time they'd been at the club, they hadn't discussed whether they would see each other again. He was asking her if she wanted more. He was daring her.

And she knew it.

Meredith didn't meet his gaze. She shook out the reins and lightly kicked at her horse to begin the ride back home. But her answer was forceful. "Yes. I plan to be there next Thursday evening."

CHAPTER SEVENTEEN

The Next Evening, The Hemworths' Ballroom

Meredith couldn't find Griffin. She knew he was here. She'd seen him and Gemma when they'd first arrived. But an hour into the ball, he was nowhere to be found. She wanted to tell them both about the dinner party she'd spent all day busily planning. She was quite looking forward to it, actually. Not only would it be a chance to further Gemma's prospects on the marriage mart, but it was an excellent diversion for someone trying desperately to stop thinking about her time at the Onyx Club with a certain gentleman with a penchant for dark-blue waistcoats.

The Onyx Club.

Meredith's entire body suffused with heat every time she thought about it. The things Griffin had done *with his mouth* last time they were there should be illegal. Of course she was quite thankful they were not. Or at least she didn't know that they were. And if they were, she never wanted to learn any differently.

THE DUCHESS HUNT

He had certainly surprised her. The man was talented both in bed and out of it. She'd had no idea he knew how to do all of those things, touch her in exactly the right spots, and lick her, and— Well, she'd learned a great deal over the last fortnight, and she wanted to continue her lessons. Which was precisely why she'd told Griffin she would be going back to the Onyx Club. She could only hope he would go back as well.

Of course, after their nearly disastrous conversation in the park yesterday, she seriously doubted the wisdom of going back to the club. But she couldn't help herself. She wanted to touch him again, wanted to feel him again. And the club was the only place she could do that…in the safety of a disguise.

She might never live down the embarrassment she'd felt when she'd realized that she'd said *Griffin's name* when he was pleasuring her while pretending to be someone else. It was madness. Thank heavens he hadn't said anything. He could have easily ripped off his mask and asked her if she'd known, if she'd always known. Instead, he'd gathered his things and left. Which was the only reason she could go back. Ostensibly, however, she should apologize to Mr. Sapphire, properly, for saying another man's name while he was touching her. And that was the reason she gave herself for why she *had* to go back to the club. She owed an apology to a man who didn't exist.

Their play couldn't go on much longer, of course. Griffin needed to find a wife, and she needed to stop her visits to the Onyx Club. It had been dangerous from the start. She promised herself: her next visit would be her last.

It had been an ill-advised adventure from the start. Oh, she'd *tried* to be worldly and sophisticated. She'd *tried* to take a stranger as a *lover*. But somehow it had all gotten twisted into something that could potentially hurt Griffin. That was the last thing she wanted to do. And now she was precariously close to ruining everything.

No. She merely needed to apologize properly, say goodbye, perhaps share one last forbidden kiss…and then she would leave the club for good. If Griffin was there, she could only hope that he would allow her to speak to him long enough to provide him with a sincere apology without trying to tell her his name again.

Of course there was another problem now. She was fairly certain that Griffin intended to ask *her* to marry him. It couldn't happen, of course. And she would have to tell him as much. Perhaps there was some way to say it before it got that far. The last thing she wanted was to hurt him. She had to somehow make him understand that she was an unsuitable wife.

She scanned the ballroom for Griffin once more. Where was he? She *missed* him when he wasn't at her side. When they'd gone for a ride in the park yesterday, she'd had more fun than she had in an age. She always had fun with Griff. Only they normally sat in her drawing room or breakfast room and read the paper and talked and sipped tea. They hadn't been out riding horses in an age. They should do that more often.

No.

A lump formed in Meredith's throat.

Griffin should do such things with his *wife*. *Not* with Meredith.

Furthermore, there would be no more guesses from her. She would simply tell him she'd run out of guesses and then begin giving him the names of ladies who would make excellent wives. Honestly, that's what they should have done from the start. Whose idea had it been to play a guessing game?

Meredith took a deep breath. Exhaling, she scoured the ballroom for Griffin one last time.

He wasn't there.

~

A QUARTER HOUR LATER, she was still searching for him. Griffin wasn't in the foyer or the drawing room. He certainly wasn't in the ballroom, and Lord Hemworth's study had been vacant when she'd walked by.

She'd already looked nearly everywhere in the house. It was time to go outside. Perhaps he was in the gardens.

She entered the Hemworths' grand library and marched over to push open the French doors that led out to the balcony that wrapped around the back of the house. When she stepped into the cool night air, a slight breeze ruffled the wispy hairs at the nape of her neck. The scent of lilies floated along the breeze. She breathed it in. Her favorite scent. She scanned the space, seeing a familiar, tall figure at the far edge along the stone balustrade. Griffin *was* there, outfitted in his all-black evening attire. He looked so handsome and so… alone.

"There you are," she called as she made her way to stand next to him. "What are you doing out here?"

He turned to her, and his face softened in the way it always did whenever he looked at her. It was comforting and familiar. Just like Griffin. She always felt safest when she was in his company. A lump formed in her throat when she thought of a day in the not-too-distant future when he would be married and no longer hers.

"Getting some air," he replied. "How is Gemma?"

"I'm happy to report that the last time I saw her she was dancing with Lord Timberly."

"Timberly? Good chap." Griffin nodded. "Is he invited to your dinner party?"

"Yes," Meredith assured him. "And she seemed to enjoy

dancing with him, though I'm certain she shall return to her wallflowers directly afterward."

His smile faded. "There's no talking her out of it if her mind is made up."

"Yes. She has the Southbury Stubborn Streak, I'm afraid."

Griffin rolled his eyes. "As if *you're* not stubborn."

"Not nearly as stubborn as you are. Here. Your cravat is askew." She reached up to fix the neckcloth for him, and the scent of his familiar cologne caught her nostrils. Their eyes met and she couldn't look away. A shudder went through her body. Was it her imagination or did a tremor go through his? She quickly fixed the cravat and stepped back, wrapping her arms around herself as she turned to stare out into the inky darkness.

She shook herself. "What were we discussing?"

"I believe you were telling me my cravat was askew," came Griffin's deep voice.

She shook her head once more. "Before that."

"You were telling me I'm stubborn."

"Oh, yes, and Gemma is equally stubborn, which is precisely why the dinner party is a good idea. If we leave it to her, she'll spend the next five Seasons finding matches for everyone but herself."

"That sounds like Gemma," Griffin replied, chuckling.

"I've sent the invitations. All to eligible bachelors, of course. And a few well-chosen ladies."

"Thank you," Griffin said, inclining his head.

"Hopefully, Gemma will use the dinner party to learn more about the gentlemen and who she is most compatible with."

Griffin lifted his brows. "You're quick to look for matches for both Gemma and me, but what about you?"

Her head snapped to face him. "What do you mean?"

"Why aren't you looking for a husband of your own?" Griffin's voice was tight, harsh.

Meredith's eyes went wide. "What? You know perfectly well that I—" God. She was as nervous as a hare in a trap. But perhaps this was just the opening she needed to make her intentions clear. "I will never marry again. *Never*."

His eyes narrowed on her. "Yes. You've said many times that you don't intend to marry again, but why is that, Mere? *Really* why?" His voice sounded nearly accusatory.

Meredith wrapped her arms even more tightly around herself. This was a subject she was loath to discuss…with anyone. Even Griffin. *Especially Griffin*. But she could tell it was more than just an attempt at changing the subject this time. He seemed almost…angry. Much like he had in the park yesterday when they'd spoken about Maxwell. "You know why," she replied quietly. "It wasn't particularly pleasant the first time."

Griffin stepped toward her, searching her face. "You made a mistake marrying Maxwell. That doesn't mean that you couldn't find love with someone else."

"Love?" Her cheeks heated. "Love?" She could barely breathe. "I stopped believing in love a long time ago."

"You've never been in love, Meredith?" His words were still a bit angry but infused with something else, something almost…sad.

She clenched her jaw. "I'm *not* having this discussion with you, Griffin." She couldn't. She couldn't have this discussion with him. Not now. Not *ever*. She shouldn't have come out here.

"That's right." He snapped his fingers. "You only talk about things that are safe. Like who *I* should marry."

That was it. She whirled to face him, her nostrils flaring. "Who says I made a mistake marrying Maxwell? You?" Why would he press her on this matter? He already knew quite well how she felt about marriage. And he knew little about the details of her marriage. She'd *ensured* he knew little about it. Why wouldn't he just accept her decision and leave it be?

But Griffin didn't back down. Instead, her words seemed to have riled him further. "Why not? You could find happiness in the arms of the right man."

She laughed. She always laughed when things got too intimate. The laugh was fake. She knew it and Griffin knew it, but it didn't matter. "You're jesting, aren't you?" She did her best to make her voice sound unaffected, but her emotions were anything but. She had to make this sound good. She had to make it sound believable. *For Griffin's sake*. "Do you know the wonderful thing about being a widow, Griffin?"

"No. No, I don't," he nearly spat.

"Freedom." She lifted her chin sharply. "I have my freedom. And I would *never* intentionally give that up."

"Freedom?" he echoed, as if the word was somehow funny.

She nodded but didn't meet his eyes.

"You only need freedom from someone who won't allow you to be free."

"Like a husband," she shot back.

"Like a *bad* husband." His eyes narrowed on her. "You know a loving husband wouldn't force you to do anything you didn't choose." He turned to her and stepped forward. His large hands covered her shoulders. His gaze met hers and held. "Really, Mere. *Why?* Why are you so dead set against marriage? You have a lot of love to give the right man. We both know Maxwell was never that to you."

Meredith bit her lip to keep the tears at bay. She pulled away from him and shook her head. She looked out into the darkened gardens, and the tears made her gaze blurry. "I was

THE DUCHESS HUNT

a terrible wife, Griffin," she whispered. "I wouldn't put another man through that."

"What? What do you mean?" He searched her profile, concern and confusion etched in his brow.

But Meredith couldn't speak. Silence fell between them for several moments. "It doesn't matter, Griffin."

"It does matter to me. Meredith, I—"

She shut her eyes and turned her head away. "Don't say it."

"Don't say what?"

"Whatever you were about to say. It won't change the past and my mind is made up. I cannot marry again. I *will not* marry again."

Griffin's voice was filled with a mixture of sadness and frustration. "Well, as you've pointed out many times, I *must* marry. But there is only one woman I can marry…because I am *madly* in love with her."

Meredith didn't wait to hear more. Instead, she lifted her skirts and ran back to the French doors.

CHAPTER EIGHTEEN

The Next Morning, The Duke of Southbury's Study

Griffin couldn't concentrate on the ledger in front of him. He'd counted the figures nearly half a dozen times already, but each time, thoughts of Meredith and their exchange on the balcony last night made him lose his concentration. It was the first time she'd ever told him anything *real* about her marriage.

I was a terrible wife. I wouldn't put another man through that.

Those words haunted him. They'd kept him up last night and kept him from balancing his ledgers today. What could she possibly have meant? She'd refused to tell him and he hadn't pressed her. He'd known she would only demur further.

Why was she convinced she'd been a terrible wife? From all accounts, it sounded like Maxwell had been an awful husband, sending her off to the country soon after their wedding and never visiting. Meredith had never told Griffin that much, but Ash had. Maxwell had left Meredith alone in the country to rot. Just as her father had during her childhood. Finding herself in that position again must have been devastating for her.

Griffin understood why she cherished her freedom. Of course he did. But a husband who truly valued her, truly loved her, would never take away her freedom. *He* would never take away her freedom. Yet she still refused to contemplate such an arrangement. And she called *him* stubborn?

She'd been young when she married, perhaps too young, but she had to know not all marriages were like what she'd had with Maxwell. The old man had practically been a stranger to her when they wed.

Of course, Griffin hadn't stayed around long enough to witness it. The day after Meredith informed him of her engagement, the day after they'd *argued* about it—Griffin had gone off to war. He'd purchased a commission in His Majesty's Army. After all, what else was the spare son good for? He'd stayed on the Continent for years. Long enough for Maxwell to die of old age.

But even after Griffin's return, Meredith's life with Maxwell was a subject she would never discuss, a barrier she would not let Griffin past. He knew there had always been something about her marriage that wasn't right. Other than the obvious. After all, it was no secret that she'd never loved Maxwell. But there was something else. Something Meredith was ashamed of. And her reticence to discuss her marriage wasn't just because Griffin had begged her not to marry the old man. There was something about her marriage she didn't want Griffin to know. And every time Griffin thought about it, he had the same notion. If that son of a bitch, Maxwell, wasn't already dead, Griffin would dig him up and beat him soundly for making her doubt herself for one moment, for causing her a second's unhappiness.

It killed Griffin to think about it. Because he knew the reason she'd married Maxwell was his fault. At least partially. He hadn't been able to stop her from going through with it. Because he hadn't told her the truth. He hadn't told her how desperately he loved her. And Griffin hated himself for that failure. Every single day. Telling her may not have made any difference, but at least she would have known the truth, and he wouldn't be in this maddening situation now.

It had been a night much like last night. Spring air. A ballroom. A balcony. Meredith, eighteen years old and ravishing in pink silk, had come in search of Griffin. He'd been out near the balustrade…alone.

"THERE YOU ARE," Meredith said when she found Griffin on the Billinghams' verandah.

Griffin turned and gave her a huge smile. "Meredith." His chest always felt less tight when she was near him. She was like standing next to a spring breeze. Fresh, beautiful, and always welcome.

"Still planning to go tomorrow?" she asked as she floated over to stand in front of him. "I cannot talk you out of it?" she teased.

"I'm going," Griffin assured her. He'd planned to go on a tour of the Continent. For years his mother had been insisting upon it, but he'd never wanted to leave Meredith. Now that she was out in Society, she seemed perfectly happy, but he was still loath to leave her.

Only he needed to go. He needed to go and return before any would-be suitors asked her to marry them. Because next year, after he returned from the Continent, after Meredith had had a Season, at the Cartwrights' Midsummer Night's Ball, Griffin intended to ask Meredith himself. But first, he wanted her to enjoy her Season. As a debutante in London, she could be young and carefree. God knew she hadn't had an idyllic childhood. She hadn't had the chance to enjoy all the pleasures London had to offer. She deserved to have fun. She deserved the best of everything. And most impor-

tantly, she'd already promised him that she'd tell him immediately if anyone proposed.

Of course, there was no reason to hope she'd say yes to his *proposal. Not yet, at least. Meredith had always treated Griffin as a friend. Nothing more. But the timing had never been right. One didn't simply declare oneself in love with one's long-time friend. There were more subtle ways to handle such delicate affairs. And Griffin had a plan.*

Once he returned, he intended to quietly court Meredith, slowly make her realize that they were more to each other than friends. It would take patience to win a woman as wonderful as Meredith. And he had patience in spades. He'd already waited all these years. What would one more hurt? He wanted to make her dream come true.

"I'm going to miss you terribly, you know," Meredith said, snapping him from his thoughts.

Griffin returned her smile. "We can write. Every day if you like."

"Of course I'll write you, Griffin. But there's something I must tell you before you go." Her pretty face clouded over.

He stepped closer and searched her visage. Something was wrong. "What? What is it, Mere?"

Her words were barely a whisper. "I'm going to marry."

A vise gripped his chest. What had she said? Marry? No. No. He must have heard her incorrectly. He cocked his head to the side, his heart thundering. "Pardon? You mean someone has proposed?"

"No. It's more than that. Father told me last night. He's already signed the marriage contract."

That sounded like Meredith's prick of a father, signing the contract first and informing his daughter of her impending marriage after the fact. But all Griffin could think of were two words. Two words that could not be true. Could not be real. Meredith...marry.

"What? Who?" he'd managed to choke out. This couldn't be

happening. One moment, he'd had all the time in the world to make things right with her, and now it was as if he were drowning, struggling for air, struggling for thoughts, let alone words.

"The Duke of Maxwell." The words shot from her lips like balls from a pistol. And they might as well have pierced Griffin's chest. They hurt so badly.

"Maxwell? You must be joking." Meredith? Marry? No.

Meredith frowned at him. "He's a duke," she pointed out. "Father said it's what Mama wanted."

A memory had come to Griffin then. A memory of fourteen-year-old Meredith sitting next to him in the grass by the pond in Surrey. They were fishing. "Father says I'm to marry a duke," she'd said all those years ago.

Damn it. Griffin hadn't thought of that day in years. He'd assumed it had just been idle talk. Something a father told his young daughter offhandedly one day. Griffin had never actually believed Lord Trentham had meant it.

Griffin reached out and grabbed Meredith by the shoulders. His fear made his grip rougher than he'd intended. "You cannot marry Maxwell," he ground out, shaking her slightly.

"What? Why?" Meredith's face was a mask of confusion.

"Your dream, Meredith? Remember your dream? A handsome young man falling to one knee at the Midsummer Night's Ball?"

Tears shone in her eyes. "You remember that?"

"Of course I remember it. You deserve that, Meredith. You deserve all of your dreams to come true."

She shook her head sadly. "That was just the silly ramblings of a girl, Griffin. You know how these things go. Marriages are often like business arrangements. Besides, Maxwell is a duke."

"You keep saying that, pointing out that he's a duke as if it means something." Disgust sounded in his voice. He could hear it. He couldn't help it.

"It does mean something," she shot back.

"I never thought it did...to you." His voice was angry,

accusatory. This couldn't be happening. He was in a bad dream, and he would wake up at any moment. "What about Ash? What does he say?" *Griffin knew he was grasping at nothing. What could Ash do to stop his father? Nothing. But Griffin couldn't just stand here and allow this to happen.*

"*Ash says it's up to me. He said he'd help me run away if I choose to.*"

"*Then run! Run, Meredith!*" *Griffin scrubbed a hand through his hair and paced away from her.*

Her angry, panicked voice sounded behind him. "*Are you mad? Ash was only jesting. I can't leave. Where would I go? I'd be ruined.*"

"*But you don't love him.*" *Griffin's voice was more severe than he'd meant it to be.*

Meredith's humorless laughter cracked off the stone balustrade. "*Love? What if there's no such thing as love, Griffin?*"

"*Marry me then.*" *The words flew from his mouth. He turned back to face her, fell to one knee, and grabbed her hand.* "*Please, Meredith, marry me. We'll go to Gretna Green. Tonight. Please, I—*"

She'd wrenched her hand from his and took a step back. "*Now who is being flippant?*" *Her face had turned to a mask of stone.* "*Marry you out of pity? Never.*"

"*It's not pity, Meredith, I—*"

"*Stand up!*" *she yelled, tears falling from her eyes. She was sobbing and Griffin's heart was breaking.*

Her tears brought him to his feet.

"*I never thought you of all people would do this to me,*" *she cried.*

"*Do what? Offer you something better than marriage to an old man?*"

"*I didn't tell you about this to ask your permission, Griffin. Nor did I expect you to understand. But I never thought you would fail to support me when I needed it. I never thought you, of all people, would make me doubt myself. Didn't you hear me, Griffin?* The contract has already been signed. *I have no choice.*"

Griffin clenched his jaw. But his fear and anger and hopelessness spurred him on. "Is that what you want? A loveless marriage to an old man you barely know?"

Meredith's jaw was clenched too, and the tears had stopped. Now, anger blazed in her storm-colored eyes. "I. Have. No. Choice. And if you cannot be happy for me, or at least pretend to be, then go." Her arm shot out, and she pointed directly toward the French doors at the far side of the verandah.

Griffin nearly crumpled to his knees then. He could think of a thousand other things he needed to say, and they all began with "don't do it because I love you madly," but he couldn't push the words past his lips because somehow, somehow he knew. Meredith would marry Maxwell no matter what Griffin said. She had already made up her mind. She would never go against her father's wishes. Even though that awful man had never deserved her loyalty, Meredith loved her father. Lord Trentham had chosen a duke for her, and she would marry him, old man or no. He'd further ensured her compliance by telling her it was what her deceased mother wanted. Lord Trentham knew precisely what he was doing.

And in that moment, Griffin realized—knew in his soul—that Meredith was lost to him. Telling her his feelings now would only make things worse for her. But he'd be damned before he would pretend to be happy for her.

"Then I'll go," he said quietly, holding his breath, filled with all the pain and longing in his heart as he turned and made his way unerringly toward the doors.

∼

GRIFFIN *HAD* GONE to the Continent. But not to travel. Instead, he went to war. For one simple reason. Because he

THE DUCHESS HUNT

was clearly lacking in courage. He hadn't even been able to bring himself to tell the woman he loved how he felt. He'd been about to say those words that night. He'd been about to blurt out how much he loved her just before she'd ordered him to stand. What in the hell had kept him from it if not fear? A coward didn't deserve Meredith's love.

Besides, would it even matter? Griffin was no duke. He was only the spare. Hadn't that been pointed out to him time and again by his father and brother throughout his entire childhood?

The sick irony was, Griffin had won many medals for courage in battle. Fought through rain, and sleet, and snow. He'd done things on the Continent he'd never dreamed of and seen things that still haunted his sleep. And there had been more than a small part of him that hoped he'd never come back. He couldn't bear the thought of seeing Meredith with Maxwell. It made his stomach churn.

Oh, he'd written her. He'd written her, and she'd written back, and they'd both pretended as if that night on the verandah had never even happened. It was their one unspoken rule. In their letters, he never mentioned the war, and she never mentioned her marriage. All nice and tidy and bloody well *fake*.

But a fake relationship with Meredith was better than no relationship at all. So they'd written about the weather, and his rations, and the latest *on dits* within the *ton*, and how the flowers were faring at Maxwell's country estate. And one day, in a letter from his mother, Griffin received the news that Maxwell was dead. Not long after, the war was over, and Griffin made his plans to return to England.

He'd rushed home, knowing Meredith would have to live in mourning for a full year, but intent on setting things straight and declaring himself the moment he could. Only when he came home, Meredith promptly informed him that she *never* intended to marry again.

And so he'd settled into life by her side once more. Content to be in her company if he could not hold her in his arms. Hopeful that one day, somehow, some way, she would change her mind.

Patience. More patience.

But now she was pushing *him* to marry. And he couldn't marry anyone but her. He'd told her as much last night. She had to have known he meant *her*. And this time, she'd run away from him.

It didn't matter. He didn't know how he would tell her or what he would say. He didn't know how she would react or how he would explain everything. For the first time in his life, he didn't have a plan.

But there was one thing Griffin knew for certain. It was bloody well time to tell Meredith the truth. At last.

CHAPTER NINETEEN

Tuesday Night, The Duchess of Maxwell's Drawing Room

The dinner for Gemma had finished not an hour ago, and after seeing all their guests to the door, Meredith and Griffin both retired to the drawing room to sit down and rest for the first time all evening.

Meredith was exhausted. In addition to being hostess for the evening, she hadn't slept a wink in three nights. Ever since the Hemworths' ball, she'd only been able to think about one thing.

Griffin was madly in love.
With her.

He may not have said it. But that's because she hadn't allowed him to. Instead, she'd run away like a coward. Because she still couldn't let him say it. He could *not* love her. He needed to love someone who could give him children, who could produce the heir to the dukedom, who could be free to love him back.

And that was the worst part. Lately, in the dead of night, when she was alone with her thoughts, she'd begun to suspect that she *did* love him back. She hadn't put much faith in love before. She'd never had a reason to. But with Griffin, it was easy, effortless even.

But even if they loved each other, it didn't change anything.

She could do nothing to encourage his feelings. In fact, she needed to dissuade him from the notion. She needed to tell him in no uncertain terms that he must pick another lady and marry her. Even though the thought made her feel sick. Not to mention, Griffin's marriage might very well put a stop to their close friendship. It *should* put a stop to it. And that was a frightening thought. Griffin had always been there for her. Since childhood. Even the years he'd been gone to war, he'd written her as often as he could. She'd always known he was there. How would she ever learn to live without him?

Thank heavens she'd had the dinner party to concentrate on these last few days. If she hadn't been spending so much time planning the perfect evening, she might have gone mad. The party had been a welcome distraction. And fortunately, tonight had been a success.

"Thank you for the lovely dinner," Griffin said as he fell onto the dark-blue sofa cushion next to Meredith.

The butler delivered two glasses of port wine and took his leave. A few candles were scattered about the room, but otherwise Griffin and Meredith sat in quiet and darkness. It was heavenly after all the activity of the evening.

"Do you truly think Gemma enjoyed herself?" Meredith asked, lifting the wine glass to her lips.

Griffin took a sip from his glass and then turned it round and round with his fingers. "She seemed to. Did you get any notion that she preferred any one of the gentlemen?"

"I truly thought Pembroke might be the chap for her, but

now I'm not certain. He does seem to be quite smitten with her."

"You're right. She didn't appear to be particularly enamored of Pembroke," Griffin agreed.

"I shall pay her a call tomorrow and ask, of course," Meredith said with a tired smile.

"Of course," Griffin replied with a nod. He took a deep breath. "Give me your feet." He set his glass on the table beside him and pointed toward Meredith's slippers.

Meredith dutifully kicked off her slippers and allowed Griffin to pull her feet into his lap. He began to massage her toes.

"Oh, my," she moaned. "That feels delightful. I had no idea you could do that with your hands." But then she blushed all the way down to her bodice.

A wicked grin popped to his lips.

Meredith closed her eyes and groaned as Griffin worked his thumb into the center of one of her stockinged feet. Oh, dear, perhaps she shouldn't have allowed him to do this. It was making her feel warm in far too many places.

"I'm glad you're enjoying it," Griffin said.

"Ooh, yes." Another moan. "That feels so good. I've been on my feet all day seeing to all the preparations."

"You must be exhausted," he replied in a deep voice, working her foot between his thumb and forefinger.

"Honestly, I am." She arched her back like a cat. "I so wanted the evening to be a success, but now I'm feeling the effects of rushing around the house all day."

"I'd say it was a success." He pulled his thumb down the center of her foot, pressing deeply.

A tremor made its way up Meredith's leg. Ooh. What he was doing with his hands should be illegal.

"How does that feel?" Griffin's voice was deep and husky.

"So good it's nearly sinful." Meredith arched her back again. "Have you always been this good at foot rubs?"

"Perhaps your feet have simply never been so tired."

"Is it getting warm in here?" She fanned her face with her hand.

"Perhaps a bit." His gaze captured hers and she glanced away first.

She let her head drop back onto the cushions and closed her eyes.

"You have one more guess, Meredith. Don't you know who she is? The lady I fancy?"

"Wh…what?" She pressed a hand to her throat.

"We've played our game long enough, don't you think?"

"It's a silly game, isn't it? I never should have started it." She was desperately trying to act as if the whole thing was hardly worth discussing further.

He tilted his head to the side and regarded her down the length of his nose as if studying her. He was still massaging her feet. "Go ahead. I know you can work it out if you think hard enough." His voice had taken on a more languid, more… sensual quality.

Meredith cleared her throat and met his stare again. The noose was tightening. "I'm…frightened." She hadn't intended to say those two words out loud, but now they were there, hovering in the air, proving to be more true with each passing moment.

Griffin's brow collapsed into a frown. "Why's that?"

Meredith swallowed. "Be…because once I make my final guess, I've little hope that you'll reveal her identity if I am wrong." It was a lie and they both knew it.

He slowly shook his head back and forth, his gaze still locked on hers. "That's not why."

She pulled at the bodice of her gown. She was sweating, and the fabric was sticking to her chest. She could barely think with him rubbing her foot that way. "Wh…what do you mean?"

"Go ahead, Meredith. Guess." His voice was languorous.

"I don't want to," she insisted, swinging her gaze away from his.

"Giving up so easily? I've never known you to be a quitter, Mere." He moved his hands to her other foot and smiled at the new groan he forced from her throat.

She expelled her breath in a long, low rush. She leaned back and placed her wine glass on the side table. "Fine," she breathed. "Lady Olivia Monthope?"

His gaze had never left hers. "No. And you knew it wasn't her."

Meredith swallowed. Of course it wasn't Lady Olivia Monthope. All Meredith had left was her misplaced anger at him for not just coming out and telling her, even though she didn't want him to. "The game is over."

"Not yet." Griffin's grin was devilish. "I have faith in you, Meredith. I'll give you one more guess."

Meredith swung her feet off his lap. She couldn't take any more of his languid foot massage. It was too intimate. Gooseflesh was spreading up her legs and giving her tremors where there should be *no* tremors. But when she pushed herself back against the sofa cushions, she found herself sitting thigh to thigh with him. And the heat from his muscled leg was scorching her. She'd never been so aware of him. His large body next to hers. The light scent of his cologne. The solid form of his shoulder so big beside hers. She closed her eyes. A tremor of desire passed through her. "I should have another dinner party for Gemma in a few weeks," she forced herself to say.

He reached for his glass. "Ah, the change of subject. A classic move in our friendship."

She bit her lip but continued to stare straight ahead. Of

course he knew what she'd done. It was what they always did. So why did it feel frightening to her tonight instead of freeing?

"Not to worry," he continued. "I know precisely how to play the subject-change game. Another dinner party for Gemma would be lovely, thank you." His smile was pat.

She lifted her chin. "I only want Gemma to be happy and find a good match."

Griffin downed more of his wine. "But not a *love* match?"

Meredith froze. She knew what he was up to. Love was a subject usually off limits for them. At least it had been ever since the night before Griffin had gone off to war. But she would not take his bait. Instead, she merely shrugged. "If Gemma thinks she's in love, all the better. I would never tell her no such thing exists."

He turned to Meredith and narrowed his eyes again. "How can you be so certain it doesn't exist?"

"You know you and I shall never agree on this topic," she replied, somewhat impatiently.

His voice was low, inquisitive. "Why, Meredith? Why are you so set on never marrying again? Why do you think you were a terrible wife?"

She sucked in her breath. "Why are you so set on discussing it?" she countered.

"Why do you think?" he countered.

"Why must you always answer my questions with a question of your own?" Her voice was nearly a whisper.

"You want to know the identity of the woman I love. I want to know why you don't believe in love. What happened with Maxwell, Meredith?"

She closed her eyes and expelled her breath. She wanted to tell Griffin the truth. She truly did. But… "I cannot tell you. It's just too…too…humiliating." She opened her eyes again.

Griffin shook his head. "We're friends, Meredith. We should be able to discuss these things."

"Don't you think I *want* to tell you?"

He shifted in his seat to face her. "Just tell me one thing then, Meredith. I need to know. Is it…does it have to do with your…intimate relations with Maxwell?"

Meredith's cheeks flamed. She pressed her fingertips to them as if to cover her shame. "Yes," was all she could manage. "Please don't ask any more."

"If there's one subject I don't want to know anything else about," Griffin breathed, "it's that. And I certainly don't want to torture you." Setting his wine glass aside, he took her hand and rubbed his thumb across the tops of her knuckles. "Let's discuss something else. If you don't believe in love, what do you believe in?"

She lifted her gaze to his and blinked up at him. "What do you mean?"

He leaned toward her and held his mouth just above her ear. "How about *passion*, Meredith? You went looking for a lover, didn't you? I assume you believe in passion."

Meredith closed her eyes and tipped her head back. He was going to kiss her. Griffin, maskless Griffin, her best friend, was going to kiss her, and of course she wanted him to.

And then his lips were on hers and there was no earthly reason she could think of to push him away. She wanted him, just as she had at the Onyx Club. She wanted him badly.

"Yes," she whispered as Griffin's hot kisses rained down her neck. "I believe in passion."

Griffin's mouth returned to hers and his lips parted over hers, coaxing out her tongue. When the kiss deepened, her arms moved up his strong shoulders and around his neck. She pulled him toward her. He leaned over her until she fell back on the sofa and his body moved into place atop hers.

Intimately fitted to his length, her fingers moved up to tangle in his soft hair.

Oh, God, yes.

It might be wrong, but this was what she'd wanted. This was what she'd been dreaming about night after night. She may have allowed Mr. Sapphire to touch her, but it was Griffin she'd fantasized about. She'd wanted him all along. No masks. No pretenses.

His mouth moved to her ear and gently traced the shell of it, while his left hand moved down to her hip. She tipped back her head, allowing him better access to her neck. He kissed slowly along the column and dipped lower to kiss her along the edge of her bodice.

He tugged on the smooth fabric and when her breast popped free, his scorching mouth covered her nipple. His teeth grazed across her bud, then he nipped it, and Meredith cried out. "Griffin," she moaned as he tugged the peak deeper into his mouth and sucked it hard.

Her core ached. Her hand moved down to touch the outline of his hard length beneath his breeches. She rubbed him up and down.

He clenched his jaw. "Meredith, please. Don't do that. I can't—"

"Make love to me, Griffin," she pleaded against his ear.

He pulled back to look into her eyes. His right arm was braced on the cushion beside her head. "Truly?"

"Yes, please," she whimpered.

Her hands were already busily unbuttoning the fall of his breeches.

"Wait, Meredith, let me make this good for you."

But she wouldn't wait. She was frantic. Mindless. This was right. She didn't want to wait any longer. She wanted him. "Now," she demanded, still unbuttoning his breeches.

Griffin helped her and soon he was free. Her hand wrapped around his thick, solid length and he groaned.

His hand went down to pull up her skirts, push aside her shift, and find her softness. He played with her folds and let one finger slowly enter her. "You're ready, Meredith. Are you certain?"

She found his mouth and kissed him hard. "I've never been more certain of anything," she said as she pressed her forehead against his, still clinging to his neck.

Griffin positioned his hips above hers and slowly slid into her.

Meredith gasped. Ooh. This was different. So *very* different from—

But when Griffin began to move, all thoughts scattered from her mind. She wrapped her legs around his hips and kissed him deeply while his hot, hard length drove into her again and again. He moved his hand down to press against her belly, bringing the soft spot inside of her into contact with his length, and when he did, she shattered into a thousand little pieces, repeating his name in a tortured gasp as waves of lust rolled through her entire body.

Griffin pumped into her again, again. "Oh, God. Meredith," he finally groaned against her mouth, finding his pleasure at last.

~

IN THE AFTERMATH, they lay in each other's arms. Her breathing came in shallow gasps. Meredith shook her head. That had been so unlike anything that had happened in bed with Maxwell. It was as if the two acts were completely unrelated.

She cleared her throat. What should she say to Griffin? How should she act now?

"We can pretend as if *this* never happened." She quirked up her mouth in the semblance of a smile. "We've had plenty of practice at it."

"You want to pretend as if this never happened?" His voice was incredulous.

"It was...amazing, but I— Of course you must marry. We don't have to tell—"

Griffin covered her mouth with a kiss and then he pressed his forehead to hers again. "Damn it, Meredith. You have one more guess. Take it. *You know*. You know in your heart who she is? You've always known."

He cradled her jaw and looked adoringly down at her face.

She broke then. She couldn't pretend any longer. Tears fell from her eyes. Perhaps she didn't *want* to know, but he was right. She did know. She *had* always known. "Me?" she whispered.

He closed his eyes briefly and kissed her again. "Yes, you. It's *always* been you."

"You...love me?" She could barely breathe. "*I'm* the lady you wish to...marry?" It wasn't as if she hadn't already guessed, but hearing it out loud, saying it out loud, made it all so...real.

He pushed himself off her, hoisted up his breeches, and fell to one knee beside the sofa. "This is hardly the way I intended to ask, but please, please marry me, Meredith. I love you. And I'll never take away your freedom." He squeezed both of her hands.

Meredith's throat was so tight it ached. This was lovely and romantic and absolutely everything at once, including... panic-inducing. But of course she couldn't marry Griffin. Even if she wanted to.

The tears would not stop. "I can't marry you, Griffin. I'm sorry. I can't."

CHAPTER TWENTY

Thursday Night, The Onyx Club

Meredith had been hiding from Griffin since the night of dinner party. But now that she was at the club, she would have to see him. And it would be easier this way. Behind masks. Still pretending. *If* he arrived, that is. And if he intended to keep up the ruse.

She'd wrestled with whether to come here tonight. What could she say? What was left to say? If he still pretended to be Mr. Sapphire, she still intended to apologize for what had happened last time. That was really all she knew.

But in the end, it hadn't even been a choice, really. She'd been compelled to come here. She *had* to know how Griffin would act.

She purposely hadn't told Griffin that she was barren. He would only say it didn't matter. She knew him well enough to know that. He would insist they marry. And she couldn't allow him to do that. Griffin was a duke. He needed an heir. He had a duty. She'd already failed the Maxwell clan. She wasn't about to be the reason *two* dukedoms remained without heirs.

Not to mention it would break Griffin's poor mother. She had been waiting for a grandchild for far too long already. The duchess loved Meredith. She would also insist they marry. No. Meredith loved them all far too much to ruin their chances of producing an heir.

She might not be able to marry him, but she couldn't forget the passion she'd found in Griffin's arms. It had been explosive, unlike anything she'd experienced before. And every second of it replayed in her mind over and over. Haunting her, torturing her.

She was already halfway through her first glass of brandy, doing all she could to block out the tantalizing thoughts of the things Griffin had said to her, the things he'd done to her body, the things he'd whispered into her ear.

Then her thoughts would flip to what he'd said afterward. He loved *her*? Of course he did. It seemed as obvious as breathing now. And she *had* known the truth. Perhaps not in her mind, but in her heart. She'd known it and had tried to make it go away, just like every other difficult emotion she'd shared with Griffin over the years.

The way he'd made love to her the first two times had been amazing, but that night in her drawing room—*that* had been unbelievable. She hadn't known that such a thing could happen. It never had with Maxwell.

"Brandy tonight?" came a deep, male voice in her ear.

Meredith turned to see Griffin standing there. He was wearing his familiar blue waistcoat and mask. So handsome. So unbearably handsome.

"Buy me another?" she asked, even though her glass was still half full.

He shook his head. "I only came here tonight to say goodbye to you."

THE DUCHESS HUNT

"Good-bye?" The word caught in her throat. She'd been planning to tell him the same thing, but the word sounded so final when he said it. Were they truly going to say good-bye to one another without admitting their identities?

"First, there's something I must tell you," he said.

She nodded. This was it. He obviously planned to tell her the truth. And she must listen and also tell the truth. "Go ahead."

"Not here." He tilted his head toward the back of the club. "Come up to the room with me? I promise I'll be a perfect gentleman."

She nodded again and waited while he paid the barkeep for the room key. She clutched her half-full glass of brandy as if it were the last shred of her sanity as she followed him up to the room. With the masks, maybe she would be able to pretend just a little bit longer.

Room seven again. Was it lucky or cursed?

When the door closed behind them, she turned to face him. "I'm glad we came up here. There's something I need to say to you too."

He pressed his back against the door and folded his arms over his chest. "Ladies first."

She took a deep breath. "I'm sorry for what happened between us the other night. It was… I was… I'm sorry." She didn't even know if she was apologizing for the last time they'd been here at the club together or that night in the drawing room. Both, probably.

"Thank you. I accept your apology," he said. "My turn?"

Meredith nodded.

∽

GRIFFIN STEELED HIMSELF. He was angry with Meredith for avoiding him all week. The morning after the dinner party, he'd tried to pay her a call. She'd refused him. Apparently, she wouldn't refuse him when he wore a mask. Somehow he'd known she would still be here tonight. And he'd been desperate to see her. That's why he'd come. But either way, it was time for both of them to stop pretending.

They needed to have this out. Which was why he'd insisted on coming up to this room. He didn't want the entire club to witness their argument. Not to mention the fact that he had no intention of removing his mask in the middle of the crowd downstairs.

Griffin took a deep breath. It was time. He was tired of living under false pretenses. From now on, he would be nothing but truthful about his identity, about his feelings for Meredith, about everything. But first he wanted some truth *from her*. And how convenient that he could ask her a few things while they were still pretending?

He stepped toward her, letting his arms fall to his sides. "Tell me something."

"Yes?" she gulped, watching him carefully.

He narrowed his eyes. "Who is Griffin? What does he mean to you?" If she wanted to keep pretending, he would let her.

"Griff, uh, Griffin is my friend. My closest friend." Another gulp. She wouldn't look him in the eye.

He continued to walk toward her, and she retreated slowly until her back hit the far wall of the small room. Then he braced both hands against the plaster on either side of her head. "Oh, I think he's more than a friend. Given what happened between us the other night. *You said his name.*"

Beneath her mask, her eyes darted from side to side as if measuring whether she could escape. She looked uneasy, and he hated that he was the one making her feel that way, but he had to hear the truth from her own lips.

"Do you love Griffin?" he demanded.

THE DUCHESS HUNT

She squeezed her eyes shut. Her pulse throbbed in her throat. "What does that matter?"

"It matters. It matters quite a lot. *To me.*" Damn her. She was still not going to give him the truth, to admit she loved him.

Opening her eyes again, she slipped from beneath his arms and hurried toward the door. When she got there, she placed her hand on the knob and paused. "I'm truly sorry to have bruised your pride. But I…must go."

"Running away?" came his mocking voice. "I didn't peg you as a coward."

Still facing the door, Meredith lifted her chin. "I'm *not* running away." She tried to sound defiant, but her voice was deflated. She knew he was right. She *was* running away.

"Where are you going then? To find *Griffin*?"

"No."

He took a seat on the bed. "Tell me. Why were you here trying to get a stranger to make love to you if you're in love with a man named Griffin?"

"I'm not in love with him!" she nearly shouted.

"Aren't you?"

She whirled to face him. "Stop! We're just friends. Griffin and I are *just friends*."

If she was going to take this all the way, then so would he. "You sound as if you're trying to convince yourself as much as me."

"I'm leaving." She turned and opened the door, but he was behind her in an instant and quickly slammed it shut again with the palm of his hand.

"No, you're not," he whispered darkly in her ear, his hand still pressed to the door. "Not until I tell you what I tried to tell you the last time you were here." He grabbed her arm and spun her around to face him as he ripped the mask off his face.

MEREDITH GASPED. She squeezed her eyes shut, and tears ran down her cheeks. "*Griffin, don't.*"

"Don't pretend any more, Meredith," Griffin growled. "I suspect you've known it was me all along."

Her silence answered for her.

He lowered his head and whispered into her ear, "And it was me. You were with *me* each time you were here, not some nameless man. You wanted *me*. I just want you to remember that, Meredith, when you're pretending we're only *friends*."

He pulled back his head to look at her. Her eyes were filled with tears, but her jaw was tightly clenched. "Griffin, why did you do this? Why did you follow me here? Why did you pretend—?"

"Ah, mock outrage?" His laugh was entirely humorless. "Did you honestly expect me to let you go to a pleasure club without ensuring your safety, Meredith? You know me better than that."

She shook her head. "You didn't have to do this. You didn't have to tell me who you are. You—"

"I what? Had to resort to a cheap device"—he flung the mask across the room—"to try to get you to admit you love me?"

She turned back toward the door. "I'm leaving."

"I don't hear you denying it though."

Her voice was low, angry. "It doesn't matter if—"

"The hell it doesn't." He scrubbed a hand through his hair. "Look, Meredith. The truth is when you married Maxwell, it devastated me. But you were dead set on marrying that old man. You actually thought you should do it for your *father*."

Her chin quivered. "My father loved me."

"Your father abandoned you and used you," he shot back.

THE DUCHESS HUNT

Tears streamed down her cheeks. "You don't know anything about my father."

"Don't I? I've heard all the stories from Ash over the years. And I've witnessed a lot of it myself."

She angrily swiped the tears from her eyes. "So what, Griffin? You think you can just tell me you love me now and I'll fall into your arms and marry you?"

"You're using your unhappy marriage as the reason you won't try again. But our marriage would be completely different from whatever happened between you and Maxwell. You *know* that, Meredith. You must know that." He captured her gaze and held it. "Now, I'm going to ask you one more time. Do. You. Love. Me?"

A steely resolve shone in her eyes. Her jaw was tight. "And I'm going to tell you one more time. *It doesn't matter*. It's too late. You'll never know how close you came to making the biggest mistake of your life. Now. I'm leaving." She ripped open the door. Her voice was low but certain. "And I never want to speak to you again."

CHAPTER TWENTY-ONE

June 1816, The Duchess of Maxwell's Drawing Room

Weeks had passed, but Meredith still didn't feel any better. She'd been sick with regret all spring. Cutting Griffin out of her life had been the hardest thing she'd ever done. But it was the right thing to do. She knew it. He needed to forget about her. He needed to find a woman who could bear him children.

He'd wanted to hear her say that she loved him. As if love was somehow a cure for all things. It wasn't. Love couldn't make her able to have children. And love couldn't fix this.

But she was also angry with him. How dare he say those things about her father? About Maxwell?

"You were dead set on marrying that old man," he'd said. *"You actually thought you should do it for your* father."

Yes. Yes to both. And Griffin, who damn well knew why she'd done it, had hurled those words at her like an accusation. He knew—she'd *told* him—that she hadn't had a choice. The papers had already been signed. The contract was already in place. It wasn't as if she'd relished marriage to an old man. She had been an eighteen-year-old girl. She didn't have the right to defy her father's wishes, even if she'd wanted to.

And Griffin hadn't stopped there.

"*When you married Maxwell, it devastated me,*" Griffin had also tossed out, as if it were an innocuous thing to say.

Had he meant that he'd loved her back then? If so, he didn't say that at the Onyx Club, and he certainly hadn't said it all those years ago. In fact, all he'd done back then was treat her as if she was a fool before making a half-hearted and, frankly, insulting offer of marriage.

She'd been devastated that night. Devastated to learn that her closest friend in the world had no intention of supporting her when she needed him most. She hadn't expected his recriminations that night. She certainly hadn't expected him to leave for years without even telling her he'd changed his plans. And now he thought a few carelessly uttered words could alter the past? As if *love* could fix everything. Love only seemed to make things worse.

The truth was she'd marry Maxwell again if she had to. Because Griffin was wrong about her father. He *had* loved her. He'd found a duke for her, precisely as Mama had wanted. Griffin hated his own father. That's why he assumed *her* father was just as awful. But Griffin was wrong. Wasn't he wrong?

A sharp knock on the door startled her from her thoughts. She closed her eyes and shook her head. "Come in," she called, expelling her breath.

The butler opened the door. "The Marquess of Trentham to see you, Your Grace."

Meredith nodded. Her brother was here. She hadn't seen him in weeks. "Show him in."

Moments later, Ash strolled into the room. He always looked perfectly put together and today was no exception.

Ash was wearing tan breeches and an emerald waistcoat with a black coat and boots. Meredith watched as he silently made his way directly over to the sideboard and poured himself a drink. Apparently, he had no intention of speaking first.

"I've been expecting you," she said.

"Really?" Ash replied in his usual good-natured tone. He splashed a healthy amount of brandy into a crystal glass.

"For weeks now, actually." She crossed her arms over her chest. "I can only imagine why you're here."

Ash grabbed his drink and came over to stand next to the sofa where Meredith sat. "Good, then I won't waste time pretending I'm here for any other reason. I've been giving you time to think." He gave her a knowing smile and lifted his glass as if in a toast.

Meredith heaved a sigh. "You're going to tell me that I have made a mistake."

"Yes." Ash nodded.

"You're going to tell me that I should marry Griffin."

"Yes." Another nod.

"And?"

Ash took a sip from his glass. "And I'm also going to tell you that you are being an obtuse, hypocritical fool," he finished.

She frowned at her older brother. "Hypocritical?"

Ash's brow lifted. "*That's* the word you take exception to?"

"Yes, actually." She tightened her crossed arms. "How exactly have I been hypocritical?"

Ash took another quick sip. "Look, Southbury has been too scared to tell you how he felt about you for years. He's been in love with you for as long as I can remember."

Her eyes narrowed. "I fail to see how that makes *me* a hypocrite."

"You're scared too. Too scared to tell him that *you* love *him*."

"I'm not scared. I'm..." She trailed off and bit her lip.

"Confused? So is Southbury. You're not the only one who can be confused, Meredith."

She drummed her fingertips along her arms. Her anger quickly ramped up again. "If he loved me so much, why didn't he tell me years ago?"

"He *tried* to tell you. The night you told him of your engagement. He said that he proposed to you that night."

"Yes, he proposed, but it was out of pity." Honestly, how could Ash not understand her anger?

"He was supposed to just blurt out how much he loved you that night after you made it clear you intended to follow Father's wishes?"

Meredith ground her teeth together. "I *had* to follow Father's wishes. I had no choice."

Ash expelled his breath and stalked over toward the window, where he took another hefty sip from his glass. "Damn it, Meredith. This has troubled me for years. I told you at the time that I would help you escape. I wasn't jesting. I never thought you should marry that disgusting old man."

"I wouldn't have run away, Ash. I would never have disobeyed Father."

"Don't you think I know that? That's the only reason I didn't abduct you myself. I knew you would have just gone back and done your duty."

"I would have," she exhaled. "Why is that so difficult for you and Griffin to understand? How can either of you blame me for it?"

Ash turned from the window to look at her again. He drained his glass and set it on the sideboard. "There's something we need to talk about after all this time, Meredith. Something I daresay neither of us has wanted to."

Meredith closed her eyes. "No. Don't say it."

"Father never loved either one of us." Ash's words weren't

filled with pain. They were simply matter-of-fact, as if he were saying nothing more important than the state of the weather.

Meredith shook her head, eyes still closed. "Mama *wanted me* to marry a duke." She opened her eyes again. They were blurry with unshed tears.

"No, she didn't." Ash stalked toward his sister, abandoning his empty glass on the sideboard. "He told me the truth, Meredith. Years after you'd married Maxwell. The old bastard got foxed and told me the truth."

Meredith's lip trembled. She shook her head. "I don't want to hear it."

Ash put his hands on his hips. "I'm certain you don't. I can't say I wanted to either, but it's time you did. The truth is that Father sold you to Maxwell when you were a girl. To pay off a *gambling debt*. He insisted Maxwell wait until you were of age, but the contract was signed when you were fourteen. Do you remember him telling you that you would marry a duke one day? It was always going to be Maxwell, Meredith."

She couldn't stop shaking her head. "Father wouldn't sell me," she insisted, but her throat closed and her stomach roiled. She felt as if she might be sick.

"Yes, he would. He did. Think about it, Meredith. What was the cleverest way to get you to agree?"

Meredith swallowed hard. She closed her eyes again. She already knew the answer, but she waited for her brother to say it.

"He knew damn well that if he told you Mother wanted it, you'd do whatever he said."

Tears trickled down Meredith's face. Ash lowered himself to the sofa next to her, pulled her into his arms, and hugged her. "I'm sorry, Meredith. It's painful to realize your own father doesn't love you."

"You've known it since we were children," she said on a sob against his shoulder.

Ash pulled back and nodded, his face grim. "Which is precisely how I know how awful it is."

Meredith took a deep breath. Ash was telling the truth. He had never lied to her. And deep down, she'd always known that she'd had to try too hard to get the slightest bit of approval from their father.

Tears poured down her cheeks. Her heart felt as if it might burst in two, and she realized the only reason she was crying was because the illusion she'd clung to fiercely for years was finally gone. And she was free to despise her father just as Ash did.

Ash was right. The man who'd given them both life hadn't loved them. He probably hadn't even liked them. He didn't even know them. How could he love them? He'd rarely come home. Rarely spoken to them. He'd treated both of his children like little more than furniture. Just two more possessions that he owned and could do with as he pleased. And Griffin had always known it too.

"You and Griffin always saw him for who he was, Ash," Meredith sobbed. "I was a fool."

"You cannot blame yourself for that, Meredith. You saw who you wanted to see. A good father. But that man never existed."

Meredith nodded. She *had* seen who she'd wanted to see —a widower who'd been lost after losing his wife. A man forced to raise two children alone and who'd done as much as he could. A loving father who only wanted the best for his son and daughter. But he was none of those things.

A memory flashed across her mind. A vision of the pure anger that had played across the lines of her father's face the night she'd tried to challenge him about her marriage to Maxwell. That harsh, unforgiving look in his eye. How many times had her mother seen that look before her death? It was too awful to contemplate.

Meredith pulled out of her brother's arms and pressed a palm to her roiling gut. "I'm sorry, Ash."

Ash frowned. "For what?" He pulled a handkerchief out of his coat pocket and handed it to her.

Meredith took the handkerchief and dabbed at her eyes. "For not listening to you all these years. For trying to convince you that Father loved us. He was…horrid."

Ash nodded. "Yes. He was. But that's why I'm here." Ash rubbed the back of his hand across his forehead. "Don't let Father make your life any worse than he already did when he sold you off to Maxwell. You have a chance for real love now, Meredith. Take it."

The hint of a sad smile curled her lips as she continued to dab at her wet eyes. "*You* believe in love, Ashford Drake?"

"No," Ash replied with a similar hint of a smile on his lips. "Of course not. Not for me. But for *Southbury*…absolutely."

A vise clenched Meredith's heart. Her brother didn't understand. How could he? "It doesn't matter, Ash. I still cannot marry Griffin."

Ash dipped his head low enough to catch her gaze. "Look, Meredith. You're scared of love. Believe me, I understand, but—"

"No, it's not because I'm scared of love." She wasn't about to tell her brother she was barren. What good would it do? Just like Griffin and his mother, Ash would only try to deny that it mattered. It wouldn't change anything, and she couldn't bear to see Ash look at her with pity.

"Meredith, please."

"There's nothing left to say. I've made up my mind. You're wasting your breath."

CHAPTER TWENTY-TWO

Later That Night, The Duke of Southbury's Study

If he thought brandy would do a damn thing to help, Griffin would be three sheets to the wind by now. But brandy never helped. And he knew for certain it wouldn't help this.

Ash, however, had no such qualms. The marquess had just poured himself a glass and taken a seat in the large leather chair across from Griffin's desk.

"What is your plan?" he asked, as if he were merely inquiring about Griffin's next move in a simple game of billiards.

Griffin frowned at him. "Plan?"

Ash braced his elbows on the arms of the chair and settled in. "You have a plan, don't you? To make things right with Meredith. You *always* have a plan."

Griffin swallowed. This awful feeling in his chest. This nausea that wouldn't go away. This feeling of being broken. This is what it felt like to know he'd ruined his friendship with Meredith.

"Seems I'm fresh out of plans," he growled at his best friend.

"Fine then. That's why I'm here." Ash took a sip of his drink. "Though I must say, between the two of you, you'll turn me into a drunkard."

Griffin leaned forward in his chair, bracing his forearms across the desktop in front of him. "You saw Meredith?"

"Indeed. Not two hours ago."

"And?" Griffin prompted.

"And it probably won't come as a surprise to you that there is no reasoning with her. She can be stubborn as a mule. She still won't admit how she feels about you."

Griffin lowered his head to his hands. "Save your breath. I know Meredith. She won't change her mind once it's made up."

Ash's mouth quirked. "Funny. She also told me to save my breath."

"She won't talk to me. Won't accept my visits." Griffin pushed himself upright again and scrubbed a hand through his hair. Damn it. Why wouldn't she admit she loved him? Why wouldn't she give him a chance?

The fact remained that Meredith had responded to *him*. She'd made love to *him*, knowing who he was. And now she was trying to pretend she hadn't felt anything. She was hiding behind her indignant anger to keep from feeling anything.

Hadn't she done the same thing the night she'd told him she was engaged to Maxwell? Ash had told Griffin how Maxwell had bartered for her, how her father had sold her like a piece of horseflesh. It made Griffin sick to think of it. He'd dig up both of those bastards and beat them to pulp if he thought either one of them would feel it.

But that didn't matter now. He only cared about one thing. Why wouldn't Meredith admit she loved him? Perhaps she didn't want to marry, not right away at least. Hell, maybe she never wanted to marry. It didn't matter to him. He'd have her any way he could. And if that was as an "arrangement," as she put it, so be it. It wasn't his preference. But he would do it. He would do anything for her.

"There's one thing she said that I can't get out of my mind," Griffin admitted, staring at his friend.

Ash took another sip. "What's that?"

"She said, *'You'll never know how close you came to making the biggest mistake of your life.'* What the hell does that mean?"

"I don't know. But I got the same impression when I spoke to her. There's something she's not telling us. Something she doesn't want us to know."

"I agree. But what could it be?"

Ash waggled his brows. "There is only one way to find out."

"You're right." Griffin leaned far back in his chair, stared at the ceiling, and expelled his breath in a long rush. An ironic smile touched his lips. He sat in silence for several long moments before he finally said, "Did you know that until my brother died, I thought I shouldn't even be alive?"

Ash winced and sucked in his breath.

"My whole life I felt as if I didn't matter," Griffin continued. "I was only the 'spare,' after all. Not good for anything but taking up space."

Ash watched him silently.

"That's why I spent so much time at your house. I always felt welcomed there by you and Meredith."

Ash nodded, contemplating the amber liquid in his glass. "We had that in common," he breathed. "The three of us were unwanted by our fathers."

"I learned to be patient. To bide my time. It was easier that way. When I was quiet or absent, Father and Richard ignored me instead of ridiculing me."

"Your father and Richard were both bastards," Ash conceded.

"Yes, they were. They're both gone now, and I'm the duke, and do you want to know something?"

Ash raised an eyebrow in question.

Griffin pushed away from the desk, stood, and planted both fists on his hips. "My patience is finally at an end."

CHAPTER TWENTY-THREE

Even Later That Night, The Duchess of Maxwell's Bedchamber

The sharp rapping on her bedchamber door startled Meredith from her troubled sleep. She sat up groggily and slowly lit the candle on the bedside table. "Who is it?" she called.

The door flung open, and Griffin strode into the room with her butler close on his heels.

"I'm sorry, Your Grace. The duke would not take no for an answer," the flustered butler explained.

Meredith closed her eyes briefly. Griffin bursting into her bedchamber was untoward, but she should have expected it. Refusing all of his visits and messages was bound to result in a display like this. Very well. They might as well get it over with. "It's all right, Jones. You may leave us."

The butler lifted a brow but nodded and left, closing the door behind him.

Meredith smoothed her hands over the pink-flowered quilt and ensured her voice remained calm. "What are you doing here, Griffin?"

Griffin looked as if he hadn't slept in days. His cravat was loose, his hair was tousled, and his eyes were red-rimmed. He pushed a hand through his hair and began pacing in front of the bed.

Meredith watched him. He was angry. That much was clear. But what precisely had he come here to say? What else *was* there to say?

"Do you know how long I've waited, Meredith? To tell you I love you?" he began, still pacing.

"No." Her voice sounded small in the large room.

"Fourteen years. At least. I counted."

She nodded, her fingers clutching the quilt so tightly her knuckles went white. "So long?"

He continued to plow his fingers through his dark hair. "Fourteen years of adoring you. Wanting to tell you how I felt. And do you know what I told myself for those fourteen years? Even during the years that you were married?"

This was more painful than she'd expected. She gulped and forced herself to ask, "What?"

"I told myself I had to be patient. To find the right time, the right way, to tell you. To convince you that we would be happy together. That we could be more than just friends."

Tears began to roll down her cheeks. "Griffin, please. Don't—"

"No. I've waited *fourteen years* and I'm tired of waiting, Meredith. I need to tell you that I've loved you desperately since I was a lad."

"Griffin, I—"

"I must finish." He paced faster. "When I was younger, I didn't think anyone would ever want me when my own *father* didn't. But now, now I've finally realized that I never told you the truth because, deep down, I thought I was unworthy of your love."

"Griffin, please—"

"I'm nearly done," he promised.

She nodded and clutched the quilt even tighter.

"Now I know that not only was I worthy of it, I always had your love, first as a friend—"

"Always as a friend," she breathed.

He stopped and gazed at her longingly. "I'm *sorry*, Meredith. I'm sorry that I followed you to the club. But I swear I only did it to ensure your safety."

She swiped at her cheeks. "That's not why I was so angry, Griffin. You were right. I knew it was you at the club. After that first night at least. And you tried to tell me."

Griffin's mouth snapped closed. He obviously hadn't expected her to say that. "Then why *are* you so angry?"

Meredith closed her eyes and took a deep breath. She forced herself to let go of the quilt, wrapping her arms around her middle instead. "You really want to know?"

"Yes, damn it. I do," he barked.

Meredith lifted her chin. "I was angry because the night you asked me to marry you all those years ago, I needed you. Not to marry me, not to save me, but to reassure me, to tell me that everything would be all right. I needed you to tell me I'd still have you as my friend, that nothing else would change. Instead, you left, Griffin. *You left me.*"

His head bowed. His voice was ragged. "I'm sorry, Meredith. If I could go back in time and change it all, I—"

"No." She shook her head and swallowed. "You were right. Father didn't love me. I never should have married Maxwell. You were right about all of it."

Griffin approached her bed and stood at the foot of it. "Damn it. I don't want to be right. I want *you*, Meredith. I've always wanted you. You know I love you. I think you love me too. I have to believe your awful marriage to Maxwell cannot be the only reason you refuse to marry again. You know I would treat you much better than he did."

She nodded, dabbing at her cheeks with the sleeve of her night rail. "You're right. It's not the only reason."

"That's why I'm here." He grabbed the poster of the bed with one hand. "You're pushing me away because you don't *want* to feel anything. Don't you see that, Mere? Denying a thing doesn't make it untrue." He took a deep breath. "You can send me away again, but I need to know *why*. I need a reason, Meredith, and I need to hear it from you."

"Griffin, I—" Her voice broke on a sob. "I can't."

His face hardened. "You say you don't wish to marry. But I need to know…is that anyone, or specifically *me*?"

Meredith tried to swallow past the enormous lump in her throat. She closed her eyes. She'd known this wouldn't be easy, but it was excruciating. "You need a wife and *children*, Griffin. We can still find someone for you. Someone who wants to marry…and have children."

His eyes narrowed on her, and he searched her face. "I don't understand. You don't want children? Is that it?"

She blinked away fresh tears. "No. No. That's not true," she whispered.

In two steps, he was at her side. He lowered himself to sit on the mattress beside her and grabbed her cold hands. "You could be with child right now, Meredith. *My child*."

She closed her eyes again and tears leaked from beneath the lids. "No, that's not poss— I know I'm not."

His voice was a desperate plea. "Then what is it? I need to hear you say that you don't love *me*."

Another sob caught in her throat. Her heart was breaking into a thousand pieces. "I can't say that, Griffin."

"Then why? *Why* won't you marry me? I deserve to know the truth."

Meredith closed her eyes. He was right. She had to tell him. She had to. "If I tell you why, you must promise to go. There will be no dispute. It is *not* up for debate."

There were a few harrowing moments of silence before one word came out of his mouth. "Fine."

She opened her eyes and stared directly into his. She expelled her breath. "I'm barren, Griffin. That's why Maxwell and I never had children. And that's why I *cannot* marry you. I *won't* allow you to throw away the possibility of an heir, even for love."

His eyes were wide as he searched her face. He shook his head vehemently. "Meredith, I don't care. I—"

"No!" she shouted. "This is why I didn't tell you before. I knew you would say that. And I *will not* be the reason the Southbury dukedom has no heir." She ripped her hands away from his. "I told you what you came here for. Now, if you truly love me, I need you to do something for me, Griffin."

"Anything," he whispered brokenly.

She pointed toward the door. "Go. Just go."

CHAPTER TWENTY-FOUR

Five Days Later, The Duchess of Maxwell's Drawing Room

"You *cannot* write me a letter like that and *not* expect me to show up at your doorstep," Clare Handleton said as she was ushered into Meredith's drawing room.

Meredith watched her friend with eyes wide. "What are you doing here, Clare? How did you manage to escape from your mother?"

Clare waved an unconcerned hand in the air. "Mother thinks I'm visiting Aunt Este in Devon, and until she writes Aunt Este and receives a reply to the contrary, she won't know any different."

Meredith gasped. "You lied to your mother?"

"It wasn't the first time," Clare said with a wink. "And I'm certain it won't be the last. I'm quite adept at it these days, actually." She settled onto the sofa next to Meredith. "Now, tell me *everything*."

THE DUCHESS HUNT

An hour later, after finishing off a pot of tea and an indecent number of scones with clotted cream, Meredith had imparted the entire tale to Clare, including the debacle at the Onyx Club and everything that had happened since. *Everything.* She spared no detail.

"You told him you were barren, and he still wants to marry you?" Clare said, nodding sagely.

"Yes." Meredith bit her lip. "Perhaps I shouldn't have told him. Only I admit now that I have, I do feel a little better… As if a weight has been lifted from my shoulders."

"Sharing secrets has a way of doing that," Clare replied with a sad smile. "I felt the same after I told you about my night with a certain nobleman who shall remain nameless."

"I never told anyone about that," Meredith hastily assured her.

Clare patted her hand again. "I know it wasn't you who spread the rumor." She sighed deeply. "But that is all long past. We are talking about *you* now. You and Griffin. And I have just one question for you."

Meredith bit the edge of her thumbnail. "Which is?"

"Do you love him?" Clare asked simply.

Meredith frowned. Her hand fell away from her mouth. "Pardon?"

"Do you love him?" Clare repeated, staring at her fixedly now.

Meredith dropped her gaze. She stared at her hands in her lap. "What does that matter?"

Clare shrugged. "Southbury was right. It matters quite a lot. And the fact that you're avoiding the question tells me all I need to know."

Meredith shifted in her seat and rubbed at her neck. "What do you mean? I'm barren. I cannot marry a *duke.*"

"I'll ask you one more time," Clare repeated, her brows raised over astute eyes. "Do you love him?"

Meredith lifted her chin and closed her eyes. "What if I do? He needs a wife who can give him heirs."

When Meredith opened her eyes again, Clare was staring at her with disbelief dripping from her countenance. "Listen to yourself, Meredith. You're saying you *cannot* marry him. You're not saying you don't want to."

"I can't marry him, Clare," she insisted. She'd made this decision already, and it was the correct one. So why did it feel like her heart was breaking all over again while explaining this to her friend?

"I'm not entirely certain about that," Clare replied. She sat up straight, knees together, and leaned forward, meeting Meredith's eyes. "Now. Because of some of the things you just told me, I must ask you something. Something that may be quite uncomfortable to answer, but I do think it's important."

Meredith nodded slowly, already dreading the question. "Go ahead."

"How do you know for *certain* that you're barren? It occurs to me that you spent many years apart from Maxwell. How many times did you lie with him?"

"Enough times to know I'm barren," Meredith quickly assured her. She had no desire to discuss the details. It was horrible enough without rehashing the past.

Clare moved even closer and covered Meredith's cold, shaking hands with both of her warm ones. She lowered her voice. "After Lord X and I spent the night together, I went the entire month *praying* for my courses. After the scandal broke, I was certain I would be further cursed by being with child."

"But you weren't with child," Meredith reminded her.

"No, I wasn't. But that didn't keep me from worrying about it for the better part of a fortnight. Mother refused to even *speak* to me, so I had to go to Aunt Este. Thankfully, she told me what I needed to know."

Meredith bit her lip. "I don't see what this has to do with—"

"Meredith, you didn't grow up with a mother. Who told you how things work, how children are conceived?"

Meredith closed her eyes. Her cheeks warmed. "No one. I just—"

"That's my point. It's possible that Lord Maxwell did not lie with you often enough to sire a child. It's also possible it was *his* failing, not yours."

Meredith shook her head. "What do you mean?"

"I mean you not having a child may not have been because you're barren."

"But Maxwell *told* me that was why. He said—" A sickening feeling began to spread through Meredith's limbs, making them numb.

Clare arched a brow. "If Maxwell was the only one telling you anything about it, no wonder you're ill-informed. Tell me. What exactly did he say?"

Meredith couldn't breathe. The words she managed came out in small bursts. "He told me…it was my fault…that he…" She glanced away, struggling to calm her breath.

"Your fault that what?" Suspicion glimmered in Clare's dark eyes.

Meredith swallowed. Clare was her close friend, but it was still humiliating to say these things. "That he couldn't…"

Clare nodded. "He didn't always—*ahem*—penetrate—did he?"

Meredith closed her eyes again. If one could die from humiliation, surely she'd have perished by now. "He would scream at me," she finally admitted. "Tell me it was my fault that he couldn't become…"

"Erect?" Clare supplied helpfully. Thank God for Clare, honestly.

Meredith nodded miserably.

"He used the word 'excited.'"

Clare took a deep breath and nodded too. "Go on."

Meredith squeezed her friend's hands. "One night, after he yelled at me, he ordered me to leave. I went to his estate in the country. I never returned. I was happier after that, away from him. He never tried to mount me again."

"I'm sorry," Clare said. "I'm sorry that happened to you, Meredith. And I suppose my scandal has left me without a *bit* of modesty. But…if he was not inside of you—"

Meredith gasped. "Oh, God. I thought Griffin and I made love three times, but the third time…the act was quite *different*. I assumed it was because I *wanted* Griffin and because he's a young, strong man."

"Listen to me, Meredith," Clare said, squeezing her hands tight again. "This is quite important. If Maxwell's manhood never hardened, if he was never inside of you, that means—"

"That means I was still a virgin when Griffin and I…" Meredith breathed. The air whooshed from her lungs as her voice trailed off. Oh, God. Why hadn't she realized this before now?

Clare winced. "Forgive me for asking, but…did it hurt at all when you and Southbury…?"

Meredith searched her friend's face. "There was a pinch. It was over quickly. And then it was…wonderful." She smiled widely.

Clare nodded. "Was there *any* blood?"

There *had* been blood. Meredith had found a small amount of what looked like blood on her shift that night. She'd asked her maid to see to it. Martha had never said anything about it.

"Yes," Meredith whispered. "But not much."

Clare pressed her lips together. "It isn't much. It happens when your maidenhead is breached."

Meredith pressed her fingertips to her mouth. "Oh, God. What sort of fool am I?"

"You're not a fool, Meredith. You're a woman who was never educated on these things. Neither was I. It's a travesty how ignorant our families allowed us to be. I would have told you myself, only I never imagined that you and Maxwell—"

"It's not *your* fault, Clare. My father should have seen to it that I had a proper education. That I had a woman to help me before my wedding, to answer questions, to guide me. I was all alone."

Clare wrapped an arm around her in a hug. "And by the time your wedding took place, I'd already been banished to the country, so I was no help whatsoever."

The two women hugged for several moments before Meredith pulled a handkerchief out of her sleeve and dried her tears. "I've spent my entire life being lied to by men. First my father, then Maxwell. Neither of them ever loved me. They were just using me. I was angry with Griffin for abandoning me, but now I know why he did. He loved me. He's always loved me. Even when I pushed him away because of another man's lies." She clenched her fists. "The time I've wasted. It makes me so angry."

"Believe me," Clare replied, "I know all about anger…and wasted time. And I know that it's absolutely useless to spend too much time with regret. The only thing that truly matters is today. What do you want *now?*"

Meredith slowly shook her head. "All these years…Griffin was right. Denying a thing doesn't make it untrue."

Clare gave her friend an encouraging smile. "You love Southbury, don't you?"

"Madly."

"Then you need to go find him and make it right."

CHAPTER TWENTY-FIVE

The Cartwrights' Midsummer Night's Ball

Meredith burst through the doors of the ballroom wearing a bright pink satin gown. She'd chosen it because it resembled the one she'd worn the night Griffin had first proposed to her…all those years ago.

She'd barely allowed Martha to dress her properly tonight. She'd been so impatient to find him. They couldn't turn back time, and they couldn't change the past, but they could start anew. If only Griffin would forgive her for being the biggest fool in the land.

"Where is the Duke of Southbury?" she demanded of the Cartwrights' butler, who was staring at her as if she'd drawn a pistol on him.

"The Duke of Southbury," she repeated in a louder, even more urgent voice. "I must find him immediately."

After looking for Griffin at his town house earlier, she'd been told that he had come here tonight with his sister. Had she been given the wrong information?

"I'm sure His Grace is enjoying the festivities in the ballroom," the butler replied, looking affronted by her rudeness.

So he *was* here. *Thank God.*

Meredith breathed a sigh of relief before thanking the butler and hurrying down the stairs. Once she made it into the crowded ballroom, she stopped at every group of partygoers. "Have you seen Southbury?" she asked, not caring one whit if the entire bloody lot of them knew how desperate she was to find him.

Suddenly, Gemma emerged from the crowd. "Meredith, what is it? Are you all right?"

Meredith grasped Gemma's forearms. "Where is your brother?" Gemma *had* to know where Griffin was.

"I believe he went out on the balcony for some air," Gemma reported, a concerned look on her face.

That's all Meredith needed to hear. Releasing Gemma, she lifted her skirts and ran toward the French doors at the far end of the ballroom. All of the ballroom's occupants turned to stare as she passed them. She was making a scene, but she didn't care.

When she made it to the doors, she pushed through them and flew out onto the balcony. Turning her head from side to side to search, she expelled her breath in relief when she spotted Griffin standing alone on the far side of the space.

"Griffin," she called.

He turned to look at her. His forehead wrinkled into a frown as she ran toward him.

By the time she reached him, she was out of breath.

"What are you doing here, Meredith?" Griffin asked. Skepticism lurked in his eyes. He was obviously guarded, careful. She couldn't blame him.

"I'm an idiot," she said between gasps for air. "I should have said yes all those years ago when you asked me. I should have told my father and Maxwell to go to hell. I should have run off to Gretna Green with you."

Griffin searched her face. His eyes narrowed. "Meredith, I don't understand. What's changed?"

"Maxwell and I… We never… In bed, we—" She still struggled to catch her breath.

Griffin sharply turned his head away. His jaw clenched. "I don't want to hear any more about Maxwell."

"You don't understand," she panted. "I thought I was barren, but now I know that when you and I made love, I was actually a virgin."

Griffin snapped his face toward her and stared at her in wonder, his eyes widening. "What?"

"It's true." She nodded. "I didn't know enough to realize that Maxwell was never…er…competent." She was blushing, but it didn't matter. All that mattered was the truth and that neither of them wasted one more second without each other.

Griffin was still watching her carefully. He took a step back. "That isn't the only issue, Meredith. You've told me many times that we were only friends. You've denied your feelings for me time and again."

She shook her head. Oh, God. She had to convince him. She had to make him believe the truth. "I know. And I'm sorry. I was confused. I was hurt. I was *wrong*."

His face remained a mask of stone as his eyes narrowed on her. "What are you saying now?"

Meredith's heart ached. He was trying to resist her. He was trying to show her that she couldn't just come running back to him and be forgiven. After what she'd put him through, she didn't blame him. Not one whit. But she *had* to convince him. Because she would die without him.

She picked up her skirts and dropped to one knee.

Griffin's eyes went wide.

"Marry me, Griffin. Please say yes. I love you *madly*."

He closed his eyes. He was warring with himself. She could tell. Oh, God. He had to still love her. He had to give her another chance. *He had to.*

"Please forgive me," she begged. "I don't know how to be in love. My only excuse is that I didn't want you to lose your only chance at having an heir. You were right. I pushed you away because I didn't want to feel anything. But I do. I do, Griffin. I love you *so much.*"

She knew the moment he'd made his choice. His eyes opened and he stared down at her with that look he'd always had for her. The one that made her feel safe and special. The one she always should have recognized meant that he adored her.

Her breath left her lungs in a solid rush as relief spread through her veins. She'd convinced him. Oh, God. She'd convinced him.

Griffin fell to his knees too. "I didn't care about an heir, Meredith. All I care about is you."

"I always knew you would say that," she said between smiling sobs. "And now I realize that we *can* have a baby. At least there's no reason to not think so."

He stood and pulled her up into his arms and spun her around. "I'm going to marry you because I love you and have since I was young. I can only *hope* we have a baby as well."

He lowered her to her feet and kissed her then, and the applause that came through the French doors startled them both. They looked over to see the entire crowd from the ballroom standing inside the glass wall clapping for them.

Meredith bit her lip and lowered her voice to a whisper. "You don't think they heard any of what we said, do you?"

"It's quite far away and the doors are closed," he assured her, his smile as bright as the sun. "I think they're clapping because we kissed."

Meredith breathed another sigh of relief. "So, you'll marry me?" She wrapped her arms tightly around his neck.

"Yes." He pulled her hands from around his neck and pressed his thumbs to the tops. "But first, I owe *you* an apology. I should have told you how I felt all those years ago. I should have been there for you when you were forced to marry Maxwell. I shouldn't have left. I couldn't bear to see you with him, but that doesn't matter. I was selfish. I'm sorry."

"And I'm sorry I wouldn't admit I loved you as more than a friend. I was scared."

"And I'm sorry that—"

Meredith put a finger to his lips. "Let's not waste any more time on recriminations, Griffin. We have each other now. Now and forever."

He pulled her into his arms and kissed her again.

EPILOGUE

London, May 1817, The Duke of Southbury's Wedding Ball

The newly married, thirty-year-old Duke of Southbury escorted his bride onto the dance floor. The crowd parted for the couple as a waltz began to play.

Meredith hadn't had *any* champagne tonight, but Griffin had imbibed *many* glasses and she'd never seen him happier. He'd especially been thrilled earlier when she shared the news that she was most certainly with child. Thank heavens the wedding was over or his mother would be scandalized. Indeed, the *ton* would be.

Meredith smiled brightly at her husband as she picked out the familiar one-two-three pattern along the floor. "You know I must confess I do miss the duchess hunt."

Griffin returned her bright smile. "And what a hunt it was." He shook his head slightly.

"One that would have been over much more quickly had I admitted the person I was hunting was myself," Meredith said with a laugh.

Griffin gave her a devilish wink. "No need to despair, my love. This Season you can turn the full force of your matchmaking skills toward Gemma. She is still in need of a bridegroom, after all."

"That's true." Meredith glanced about. "Speaking of Gemma, where *is* she? I was hoping she'd dance with Lord Timberly tonight."

"I just saw her a few minutes ago. She asked me if I'd seen Grovemont, actually."

"Grovemont?" Meredith frowned. "Hmm. I wonder why."

"I've no idea. But—"

"Southbury! Southbury, come quickly!" a shrill female voice called.

Griffin and Meredith stopped dancing as Lady Cranberry came hurtling toward them through the crowd, waving her embroidered handkerchief in the air like a flag.

"What is it, Lady Cranberry?" Griffin asked. He and Meredith stared intently at their guest, waiting for her to explain herself.

"You must hurry," Lady Cranberry shrieked. "Your sister was just discovered alone in the study with the Duke of Grovemont!"

∽

THANK YOU FOR READING. I hope you enjoyed Meredith and Griffin's story. The next book in the Love's a Game trilogy is *The Duke Dare*. Find out what Gemma was doing in the study with Grovemont. CLICK HERE FOR *The Duke Dare* now.

ALSO BY VALERIE BOWMAN

Love's a Game
The Duchess Hunt (Book 1)
The Duke Dare (Book 2)
The Marquess Match (Book 3)

The Whitmorelands
The Duke Deal (Book 1)
The Marquess Move (Book 2)
The Debutante Dilemma (Book 3)
The Wallflower Win (Book 4)

Lords in Disguise
The Footman is an Earl (Book 1)
Duke Looks Like a Groomsman (Book 2)
The Marquess Who Loved Me (Book 3)
Save a Horse, Ride a Viscount (Book 4)
Earl Lessons (Book 5)
The Duke is Back (Book 6)

Playful Brides
The Unexpected Duchess (Book 1)
The Accidental Countess (Book 2)
The Unlikely Lady (Book 3)
The Irresistible Rogue (Book 4)
The Unforgettable Hero (Book 4.5)
The Untamed Earl (Book 5)

The Legendary Lord (Book 6)
Never Trust a Pirate (Book 7)
The Right Kind of Rogue (Book 8)
A Duke Like No Other (Book 9)
Kiss Me At Christmas (Book 10)
Mr. Hunt, I Presume (Book 10.5)
No Other Duke But You (Book 11)

Secret Brides

Secrets of a Wedding Night (Book 1)
A Secret Proposal (Book 1.5)
Secrets of a Runaway Bride (Book 2)
A Secret Affair (Book 2.5)
Secrets of a Scandalous Marriage (Book 3)
It Happened Under the Mistletoe (Book 3.5)

Thank you for reading *The Duchess Hunt.* I hope you enjoyed Meredith and Griffin's story.

I'd love to keep in touch.

- Visit my website for exclusive information about upcoming books, excerpts, and to sign up for my email newsletter: www.ValerieBowmanBooks.com or at www.ValerieBowmanBooks.com/subscribe.
- Join me on Facebook: http://Facebook.com/ValerieBowmanAuthor.
- Reviews help other readers find books. I appreciate all reviews. Thank you so much for considering it!

Want to read the other Love's a Game books?

- The Duke Dare
- The Marquess Match

ABOUT THE AUTHOR

Valerie Bowman grew up in Illinois with six sisters (she's number seven) and a huge supply of historical romance novels.

After a cold and snowy stint earning a degree in English with a minor in history at Smith College, she moved to Florida the first chance she got.

Valerie now lives in Jacksonville with her family including her two rascally dogs. When she's not writing, she keeps busy reading, traveling, or vacillating between watching crazy reality TV and PBS.

Valerie loves to hear from readers. Find her on the web at www.ValerieBowmanBooks.com.

- facebook.com/ValerieBowmanAuthor
- instagram.com/valeriegbowman
- goodreads.com/Valerie_Bowman
- bookbub.com/authors/valerie-bowman
- amazon.com/author/valeriebowman

Printed in Great Britain
by Amazon